Booth's Daughter

Booth's Daughter

Raymond Wemmlinger

CALKINS CREEK

Honesdale, Pennsylvania

LIBRARY OF CONGRESS CATALOGING-IN-PUBLICATION DATA

Wemmlinger, Raymond.
Booth's daughter / Raymond Wemmlinger. — 1st ed.
p. cm.
Summary: In nineteenth-century New York City, Edwina, daughter of the
famous actor Edwin Booth and niece of John Wilkes Booth, finds it
difficult to escape the family tragedy and to meet the needs of a demanding
father while maintaining her independence.
ISBN-13: 978-1-932425-86-4 (hardcover : alk. paper)
[1. Fathers and daughters—Fiction. 2. Booth, Edwin, 1833–1893—Fiction.
3. Actors and actresses—Fiction.
4. New York (N.Y.)—History—19th century—Fiction.]
I. Title.
PZ7.W46889Boo 2007
[Fic]—dc22
2006012073

Calkins Creek
An Imprint of Boyds Mills Press, Inc.
A Highlights Company

815 Church Street
Honesdale, Pennsylvania 18431

11/07   47.95

Booth's Daughter

ONE **1880**

The one play Papa performed that he would never let me see was *King Lear*. "Too harsh for a young lady," he said. Over the years I had gradually seen *Hamlet, Othello, Richelieu, The Fool's Revenge*, and the others. Papa always felt strongly that children should not be exposed to subjects too mature for them. But when it was announced that he would open his March 1880 New York engagement with *King Lear*, I pointed out to him that I was now eighteen, quite old enough to see it. He didn't object, but I really hadn't expected him to. He had been treating me as an adult since I had finished school and returned to live with him and Mama, my stepmother.

Papa's appearance at Booth's Theatre would be an event in itself: for the first time since he had lost it in bankruptcy, he was to act on the stage of the theatre he had built. Papa had said he would never perform there again. He had been especially bitter over being legally unable to prevent the new owner from using the old name. But the theatre had now changed hands again, and Papa's manager, Henry E. Abbey, had been offered very generous terms for Papa's appearance. The shrewd idea of coupling it with an infrequently performed play had been Mr. Abbey's. "The public will pack themselves in," he told Papa. I was not surprised when I entered my box for the opening-night performance to find the immense theatre filled nearly to capacity.

As always, faces turned up to me when I came in, people curious to see the star's daughter. I had perfected a smile for such occasions: serene, proud, and expectant. I was not only Edwin Booth's daughter, his only child, but also his greatest admirer.

"This is still the grandest theatre in New York," said my friend Julia as we sat down.

I silently agreed. I was glad the theatre was still called Booth's, glad that long after Papa was gone this beautiful building would stand as a reminder of the great artist who had built it. But I said soberly, "It cost far too much to build, Julia. Papa was never able to recover from the expense. His partner turned out not to have been much of a gentleman."

I hoped these few remarks would be enough to deflect any further discussion of the loss of the theatre, as they usually were. But Julia blurted out, "Edwina, doesn't your father feel at all awkward playing here now? Or sad?"

To conceal my discomfort, I glanced down at my fan. It was foolish for me to deny that this very question had been in everyone's mind since the announcement that Papa was to appear at Booth's, but no one had been thoughtless enough to bring it up to me directly. Julia, however, was notorious for saying the wrong thing at the wrong time. Aside from that, she was kind and cheerful, and a good friend. For all her bluntness, she had always known not to ask me about what Papa and I referred to as "The Subject." Had she done so, I would have given my usual response in a chilly tone: *My unfortunate uncle John Wilkes Booth died when I was three years old. I remember nothing of him.* Then I would have distanced myself from her.

Although it was not strictly true that I had no memory of my uncle, it *was* true that I knew nothing of President Lincoln's assassination. Papa never discussed it, and he would make only the most oblique references to his brother. Most people understood that this was not something we cared to talk about. Occasionally someone would bring it up. During my years at school, more than one budding friendship had ended abruptly.

Tonight, Julia was excited to be at Papa's opening, and I couldn't blame her for asking something many people were thinking. I gestured down to the stage. "The beauty of the building is what is important, Julia. More important than Papa owning it."

"That's how my father feels about the park!" Julia said. Her father was Calvert Vaux, the landscape architect who with Frederick Law Olmsted had designed New York's Central Park. "You know, Edwina," she added, "we have so much in common that we could be sisters!" She smiled mischievously. "And perhaps someday we will be."

"Oh, hush, Julia!" With studied poise I opened my fan and began to use it. "You make something of nothing. Your brother is too involved in his work to indulge in nonsense."

"Downing speaks of you often."

"A few polite attentions ..."

"No, it's more than that. Today he told me that he feels you and he have similar ideas about life. He'd like to see more of you."

The fan slipped from my hand. I bent to retrieve it while Julia laughed, her mass of dark curls bobbing.

"Oh, Edwina, you're such a schoolgirl! Well, Downing will be at the supper tonight. You can see for yourself!"

I fanned myself vigorously. The possibility that Downing Vaux was interested in me was beyond any serious hope on my part. The recent months had been something of a social whirl for me, and I had met many young men. In June I had finished my studies at the convent school near Philadelphia that I'd attended since childhood, and this past winter had been my first season in New York City. I was nearly overwhelmed with invitations to social events, teas, suppers, dances, musical evenings, and many parties just for young people. Most actors were not viewed as acceptable in polite society, so I had not expected to be included, but apparently Papa, because of his great talent and dignified demeanor, had always been an exception. I found myself being paid quite a bit of attention, especially by young men. Unfortunately, most of them were boys, really, and rather foolish. None of them had any great goals or ambitions. In my opinion, parties and dances were fine, so long as one remembered that life was serious business. Few young men seemed to realize that.

But Downing Vaux was different. About ten years older than I, he stood far above the other young men. His maturity was a delight; he was serious, intelligent, and sensitive. Most important, he had aspirations to be an artist, to make some creative contribution to the world.

"You do plan to come tonight?" asked Julia.

"Yes."

"You're certain?" she pressed. Evidently, the prospect of a romance between her brother and me pleased her enormously.

Before I could assure her that it would please me just as much, the house lights began to dim. The audience hushed, and a great silence, rich with expectancy, settled over the theatre as the darkness became total. Then the curtain rose on a stage full of light, and *King Lear* began.

Within minutes Papa appeared, heavily made up to resemble the old king. A great burst of applause greeted his entrance.

A familiar rush of pride came over me. No doubt the heavy applause that always accompanied his appearance contributed to this sensation, and tonight that applause was thunderous and prolonged.

As the wave of applause began to recede, Julia leaned over and whispered, "How old he looks!"

"It's only makeup," I whispered back, a little defensively, for I had been thinking the very thing myself. I studied Papa carefully. He was only forty-seven, but tonight he'd been made up to look eighty. Even so, his face was still radiant, full of charisma, the unmistakable quality of a star, which eluded so many lesser performers. And a moment later, when he began to deliver his first speech, the entire theatre was filled with the compellingly rich tones of his voice. Here was Edwin Booth, tragedian beyond compare.

By the first intermission I had decided that I disliked the play. It was all well done, especially Papa's performance, but the play itself struck me as distasteful. The character of Lear lacked the princely dignity of Hamlet or the powerful majesty of Cardinal Richelieu. And to think that for years I wondered what terrible mysteries this play held! I hoped that in the future Papa would not choose to revive *King Lear* more frequently, but the loud applause that greeted the intermission told me that he might. The audience was clearly pleased with Edwin Booth as Lear.

I stifled a yawn as the lights came up; it would never do for the daughter of the star to be seen looking bored. Once again the great theatre sprang to life, filled with excited, chattering voices. The vast orchestra section became a sea of movement, the colorful evening gowns of the ladies swirling around the black formal wear of the men.

There was a polite knock on the door of the box, and Henry Flohr, Papa's backstage dresser, came in. Henry was a tall, bony, white-haired man who had first worked for Papa back in the days when Papa owned Booth's Theatre. I hadn't seen him for six years.

Wide-eyed, he stared at me. "Little Edwina! Little Edwina!" he murmured. "I can scarcely believe it's you!"

I smiled at him. It was a genuine pleasure to see him, although I couldn't help but notice how much he had aged. "I'm all grown up now, Henry."

"So I see." He continued to stare at me. "Forgive me, but I look at you and see your mother."

Delighted, I beamed at him. This had always been the highest compliment someone could pay me. My mother died when I was one year old, but I had photographs of her in which her beauty was evident. Although the dark coloring and sharp angularity of feature of the Booth family were strikingly attractive, I had always been pleased that I took after my mother, with my light brown hair and softer facial features. I did resemble Papa in that my best feature was my eyes. But where his were dark brown and sad, mine were a hazel gray.

Henry handed me a note on a folded piece of paper, a message from Papa. Then he patted me on the head, because I was still "little" Edwina to him, and left. The note, in Papa's slanted, heavy writing, asked me to stop backstage after the performance. What it really meant was that Papa thought Mama's nervous condition was manageable tonight, so my appearance in the dressing room would not be likely to bring on an attack.

"Julia, I must see my father for a few minutes after the performance."

"Backstage? May I come?"

I hesitated. My stepmother's moods could change in an instant. One never knew what would set her off. Julia would be thrilled to go backstage, I knew, but it was too risky to take her. I decided to speak honestly. "Julia, dear, you know Mama hasn't been well lately. Sometimes a crowded room disturbs her."

Julia reached over and patted my arm. "Of course."

"You go ahead to the supper, and I'll come along later."

When the play finally ended, several long hours later, there were nine curtain calls, and cheers, and cries of "Bravo!" Everyone but me was thrilled with the evening's entertainment. But I now liked the play no better than I had earlier. I thought the multiple deaths at the end were disgusting.

As we left the box I told Julia to run along to the supper party in Gramercy Park. Once again she asked if I really meant to come. I assured her I did.

"Downing does care for you, Edwina," she said, speaking quickly and with unusual urgency. "So please, please, come tonight!"

I smoothed down the fur collar of her wrap. "Silly goose, I wouldn't miss it for the world. But first I must see Papa."

Papa was speaking to a plump, middle-aged man when I entered the dressing room. He had changed into a black robe and was seated at his dressing table removing the last traces of Lear's makeup.

In the mirror he saw me. "Ah, here is my daughter." He rose and came to me. I saw he had the sense of exhilaration that meant he was pleased with his work.

"A beautiful performance, Papa." I kissed his cheek.

He gave my arm a little squeeze. "Edwina, this is Mr. Neville. From Philadelphia."

Mr. Neville bowed low in a grand manner that instantly told me he was an actor. "I come a humble suppliant to your father."

"Mr. Neville comes on behalf of the Actor's Order of Friendship."

From the adjoining sitting room, Mama shrieked, "Edwina! Come meet Mr. Grossmann!"

"My brother," said Mr. Neville.

"Go," Papa said softly to me. "We will speak later. Or have you plans?"

"I'm expected at a supper …"

"Tomorrow, then." He smiled at Mr. Neville. "The energy of the young for socializing never fails to astonish me."

"Oh, Papa."

"Edwina!" The call was a shrill command.

"Go," said Papa.

Mama was serving tea to a fair-haired, smiling young man with a wide mustache who seemed to be enjoying her chatter immensely. For a moment I stared. It was highly unusual for Mama not to be glued to Papa's side. And seldom did she respond well to strangers.

"Edwina, don't just stand there! This is Mr. Grossmann. Mr. Ignatius Grossmann. Mr. Grossmann, my daughter, Edwina."

He jumped up and bowed briskly. He was younger than his brother, probably in his late twenties, and of a more slender, compact build. His pleasant, wide face was framed by long side-burns. Just as I had known that his brother was an actor, I knew at once that he was not.

"Mr. Grossmann speaks seven languages, Edwina. Seven!"

"Not all very well, I'm afraid." His voice held the barest trace of a central European accent.

"Sit down, Edwina. Have some tea with us."

"I really can't, Mama."

"Yes, you can."

Hearing the petulant tone in her voice, I quickly sat down and undid my cloak. If Mama was in a rare good mood, I would not disturb it. Perhaps she was even starting to get well.

I looked at her pale face and small figure and felt a genuine affection and concern. Mama was little more than a decade older than I. As usual, she was perfectly dressed in the most stylish current fashion, and her hair was nicely arranged. No matter how disturbed and unreasonable she became, even in her darkest moods, Mama's makeup and attire were always perfect.

Mr. Grossmann sat down again. "How nice of you to spend a few minutes with us, Miss Booth." An air of good spirits radiated from him.

Mama thrust a cup of tea in front of me. "Edwina studied languages at school. She speaks French! What are the others, Edwina?"

"German and Italian. A little Latin."

"Where did you go to school?" Mr. Grossmann asked.

"St. Mary's Convent, outside Philadelphia."

"Mr. Grossmann used to teach languages, Edwina."

"Oh?"

"Yes." He smiled at me. I noticed his eyes were hazel, as were mine. "At a college that is, coincidentally, also outside Philadelphia."

"But now he makes money!" said Mama, laughing.

Embarrassed, I stared into my tea. But Mr. Grossmann laughed also. "Yes, I confess I have changed to a money-making profession. I am now a stockbroker here in New York."

"I see." I sipped my tea. It was odd that he could view with levity his unfortunate career change. Teaching was such a noble profession!

The tea was lukewarm, and bitter. Without thinking, I reached for the small bowl of sugar in the center of the table.

"*Edwina!* No sugar!" Mama screeched.

Quickly I withdrew my hand.

Mama's posture had become rigid. "How many times must I tell you? *Young ladies do not use sugar!*"

Please do not let her start, not in front of a stranger, I thought desperately. My mind raced for a way to pacify her, but without success.

"Mr. Grossmann, Edwina is very, very forgetful! Very! I try so hard to teach her things, but she simply forgets!" Mama's small eyes narrowed. "Or she *says* she forgets. Sometimes I think she just ignores me! *Ignores* me, after I try so hard!"

Mr. Grossmann glanced at me. "But, Mrs. Booth, how very fortunate she is to have you to guide her! You who are so socially adept, so gracious. And so wise. I can't tell you how much I've been enjoying our little chat here today! Miss Booth, your mother has been telling me about her splendid autograph collection. How fascinating it sounds!"

At once the stiffness drained from Mama's posture. She began to chatter excitedly about the collection. Mr. Grossmann listened attentively, his pleasant face arranged in an expression of deep interest.

I felt a surprised admiration. He had managed Mama with more ease and deftness than Papa was at times able to summon. I reviewed his words to determine the key to his success. He had created a distraction, changed the subject, but Papa did that frequently. Sometimes it worked; often it did not. There had been something else.

Flattery. Mr. Grossmann had flattered Mama, offered her praise. And she had devoured it as though starving. I leaned back in my chair and sipped my bitter tea.

A few minutes later Papa and Mr. Neville appeared in the doorway. Papa was lighting one of the short brown cigars he smoked incessantly. "The Actor's Order is a worthy organization that I greatly respect. I would like to do something. If you will call at my hotel, the Brunswick, tomorrow afternoon, a check will be waiting for you. A small donation. And perhaps when I return from Europe I can be of further help."

Hearing this, Mama forgot her autographs. "Mr. Grossmann, Mr. Booth is going to be appearing in London soon. It's high time he played there again!"

Politely Mr. Grossmann asked, "Do you like London, Mrs. Booth?"

"I've never been there. Mr. Booth played there before … before …" Her voice drifted to a halt, as though something of overwhelming urgency had just swooped into her mind. With the disoriented look of a person suddenly awakened from a nap she glanced around the room. Her gaze came to rest on Papa. A second later she stood rigidly at his side, her arm linked through his. Her eyes had become distant.

Mr. Grossmann had stood up when Mama had, and he and his brother were now slipping on their overcoats. I began to button my cloak. "Papa, I must go."

"Yes, you cannot be late. I'll have Mr. Flohr get you a carriage."

At once Mr. Grossmann said, "I would be happy to see Miss Booth to her destination."

I stood up. "Thank you so much, but it's really not necessary. I don't wish to trouble you."

"It's no trouble. On the contrary, it would be a pleasure."

"Mr. Neville will be inconvenienced."

Mr. Neville laughed. "Not at all, my dear, although it is kind of you to think of me. I have others to confer with this evening, and my brother would only be bored. Ignatius, do escort Miss Booth."

I looked helplessly at Papa, who had remained silent all through this exchange. A cloud of cigar smoke around his head caught the gaslight and created an eerie halo. Before he could speak, Mama startled us all by commanding, "Edwina! Go with Mr. Grossmann!"

There was an awkward silence before Papa said quietly, "So it's settled."

Mr. Neville said good-bye and left. I kissed Papa and Mama good-bye.

Mr. Grossmann bowed to Mama, saying, "Mrs. Booth, thank you so much for tea and a delightful conversation."

"You're welcome," she answered dully.

"Mr. Booth, it is a great honor to have met you. And may I once more praise your personification of Lear."

Papa bowed. "Thank you, sir."

In front of the theatre Mr. Grossmann helped me into a carriage, then settled in beside me and asked me for the address of the supper party.

"Number Six Gramercy Park West," he called to the driver. "Then uptown." As the carriage pulled away from the sidewalk I felt obligated to invite him to join the party. To my relief he refused, pleading the need to rise early in the morning. "To make money," he added playfully.

The carriage started off across Twenty-third Street, the

horse trotting at a leisurely pace. I wished it would go faster, for I felt awkward with Mr. Grossmann.

"Did you enjoy the play?" he asked.

"Yes," I lied, staring straight ahead. "I enjoyed it very much."

"I did not," he said frankly. "That play is much too grisly for my taste." He paused. "You know, for many years it was performed with a different ending. A happy one."

"Oh?" I looked at him.

"Lear and his good daughter survive. She marries Kent, and they live happily ever after. I would prefer that ending."

I decided I would ask Papa if this was true.

"But your father's performance was excellent. He is a great, great actor. As was his father in his day."

"Yes." My grandfather Junius Brutus Booth had been one of America's first important actors.

"Miss Booth, may I ask …"

For one dreadful moment I thought he was going to bring up The Subject. The last thing I wanted right now was to have to fend off his questions about John Wilkes Booth.

But that wasn't his question. Instead he asked, "Have you no desire to act, yourself? Carry on the family tradition?"

I relaxed a little. "No, I'm no artist. Which I do believe actors are."

"Certainly."

"I'm glad you agree. Oh, yes, of course—your brother is one … It's appalling how many people today still think actors are little more than circus performers! But no, acting's not for me."

"What is, then?"

"I can see myself as the wife of an artist, devoting myself to his career. My mother did that. She was an actress, but she left the stage when she married my father. My stepmother did the same." I frowned as I recalled Mama's behavior. "She's not well, you know. My stepmother."

"I enjoyed meeting her."

Was he joking, or patronizing me? No, his tone was sincere. He had enjoyed it. I said, "You can't imagine how it disturbs me seeing her this way. I was seven when I first met her, and I thought I was meeting a princess."

Why was I telling him this? Confiding in a near stranger? Yet I continued, "Her nervous illness, the irrational moods and suspiciousness, began when my brother died at birth. She never fully got over it." Mama had become pregnant right after her marriage to Papa. She had nearly died trying to give birth, and in the end her life had been saved only by crushing the infant's head with forceps. They had named the little boy, who had lived less than an hour, Edgar.

"A tragedy," said Mr. Grossmann.

"Yes," I said. It occurred to me that Edgar was the name of an important character in *King Lear*. I wondered if this was why my parents had chosen it.

The carriage stopped briefly in Madison Square while a horse-drawn rail car passed in front of us. Then we continued east toward Lexington Avenue.

"So you would devote yourself to art through your husband's career?"

"Yes. It seems the noblest thing a wife can do."

"The wife of an artist."

"Yes."

Mr. Grossmann considered this for a moment. "But what of happiness?"

"Well, I should think I would be happy. And so would my husband."

To this he said nothing. My earlier discomfort with him began to return.

The carriage started down Lexington Avenue and a few moments later turned in at the square of tall townhouses surrounding Gramercy Park. The west side of the square was the most attractive, with a great web of decorative iron porches, gates, and railings spread around the entrances and lower windows of the houses. The windows of Number Six were full of light, and the carriage stopped before it. Mr. Grossmann stepped out and held the door open for me.

"Miss Booth, it has been my pleasure. I hope you enjoy your evening."

Above the stoop the door to Number Six was opening to receive me. "You were so kind to see me here, Mr. Grossmann. Thank you. Good night."

"Good night," he said, jumping back into the carriage. It pulled away from the curb and vanished around the corner of the park.

I hurried up the steps and into the shadowy hallway of the house. As the door closed behind me one of the male guests came out from the brightly lit drawing room to greet me. The light behind him shadowed his features, and I could not make out who it was.

"At last, Miss Booth," he said, and I recognized the soft voice of Downing Vaux.

The windows of my room on the fifth floor of the Brunswick Hotel in Madison Square faced east, and the late-morning sunlight streamed in when Betty, my maid, woke me by opening the drapes roughly.

"Time to get up, missy," she said. "You can't sleep all day even if you were out dancing all night."

I peered up through heavy lids at the ebony-skinned, red-kerchiefed woman towering over me. "I wasn't dancing," I protested feebly. "And I wasn't out all night."

"I know just what time you came in!" she said. Indeed she did; I had been confronted by her furious figure when I arrived home at 2 a.m. "I was ready to go for the police," she had hissed before storming out of the room, leaving me to get ready for bed by myself.

Any perceived threat to my safety was the surest thing to bring on Betty's wrath. Normally quiet, at those times she revealed a sharp vocabulary that would strike at whoever or whatever had been unfortunate enough to incur her rage.

"Your dress has got mud on it!" she said now.

"Mr. Vaux walked me home from Gramercy Park. The streets were muddy."

"What kind of a gentleman lets a lady walk in mud?"

"He's very, very nice."

"Where are your shoes, or did you just throw them right in the trash? Mr. Booth's going to have to start acting three times a day to make enough money to keep up with you, missy! And you say you *walked* here! At that time of night! Lucky you weren't killed, missy! If it were up to me, we'd go straight back to St. Mary's!"

I sat up. Betty had been happy in the sheltered, quiet convent school that had been our primary home for twelve years. Although there had been frequent vacations away, sometimes for extended periods, the comforting stability of life at St. Mary's always hovered in the background. Betty did not feel as safe in New York City as she had felt there, and I knew she lamented the fact that St. Mary's was gone forever from our lives. That same fact, however, caused me no more than the tiniest twinge of regret. I was happy to finally be out in the real world.

But I would have to be more sympathetic to Betty and help her adjust to our new circumstances. "Betty," I said, "I'm sorry you were upset; I should have warned you I'd probably be late. But it really was safe walking home. It was peaceful, so quiet."

"The morgue's quiet too," she muttered. "Well, hurry up now. Mr. Booth ordered down for breakfast a few minutes ago." She went into the bathroom, and I heard her turn on the water in the tub. Then she reappeared in the doorway, hands on her hips. "Who's this Mr. Vaux?"

"Julia's brother. Papa's friend Mr. McEntee is his uncle."

"What does he do?"

"He works for his father now, but he's going to be an artist, a painter. He's very talented!" I threw back the covers and slid my bare feet out of bed and into a pool of sunlight on the carpet. "And he's very intelligent!"

"How come he made you walk home? He short on cash?"

"He didn't *make* me walk, Betty! He suggested it so we could talk. The supper was noisy."

"Talk? What about?"

"Oh, everything! He's so poetic. Very different from most men."

"Men are all the same." Betty had been married once, but her husband was gone by the time she came to work for my family. I didn't know the reason for his absence, but Betty's occasionally voiced low opinion of men led me to assume that those reasons were not pleasant. Betty never married again, or had a boyfriend or companion, although she had been young enough, and attractive, with the face and body of a Nubian queen. Even today, despite the shapeless dark dresses she always wore, I had seen her draw appreciative glances from men, and once or twice heard them venture remarks. But these would-be admirers were always swiftly discouraged by Betty's acid tongue.

"Well, when are you going to see him again?"

"This afternoon. We're going to an exhibition."

"Mr. Booth know him?"

"Not yet. But he will soon."

"I ought to make you wear this muddy dress to that exhibition," Betty grumbled. "And I would if it weren't an evening dress." She disappeared into the bathroom.

"I'm sorry about the mud," I called after her.

Papa and Mama's suite lay directly across the corridor from my room. It consisted of two bedrooms separated by a spacious sitting room where our meals were served when we chose not to eat in the hotel's frequently crowded dining room. The Brunswick's reputation for luxury was upheld by the suite's elegant furnishings, all red and gold, and polished mahogany.

Breakfast was waiting by the time I came in, the covered silver dishes gleaming on the small cart. Papa had already finished eating but was still seated by the window at the large table that we used for meals. He was opening the morning mail, which lay in a small pile in front of him, along with a stack of newspapers and a half-finished cup of coffee.

He looked up from the letter he was reading as I came in. "Good morning, darling."

"Good morning, Papa." I kissed him on the cheek. "Mama's not up yet?"

"She started coughing again last night." During the winter, Mama had developed a cough that stubbornly kept reappearing. It usually struck when she retired, keeping her awake far into the night. Consequently, she slept late the next morning, some-times into the early afternoon.

"She seemed a little better at the theatre yesterday," I said, hoping he would agree. But when he didn't reply, I let the subject drop. My eye caught the stack of morning newspapers. "How are the reviews?"

"See for yourself," he said with a little smile.

The stack included all the New York morning papers, including the *Tribune, Times, Star, Herald, World,* and *Truth.* I picked one up, found the review, and read it.

It was a rave review, not only for Papa but for the entire cast as well. I was sure all the other reviews would be in a similar vein. Although I had not liked the play, I was relieved by its recep-tion. Most of the time Papa was capable of simply shrugging off a negative review. But on one occasion that I would never forget, a bad review had caused him to sink into a dark mood so overwhelming he was nearly unable to finish his engagement. It happened during one of my school holidays, and I had watched as Mama strove heroically to bolster Papa's spirits, ultimately enabling him to honor his commitment. "Don't worry, Edwina," she told me. "Everyone becomes that way sometimes." And I hadn't worried. But that was a long time ago, in the early stages of Mama's own illness. Mama's intervention would be out of the question should there be a recurrence now. Luckily, there had never been one since Mama's own nervous illness had become more overt, even through the awful days when Booth's Theatre was lost. It was as if Papa was not permitted to be ill while Mama required so much of him.

But the reviews were good. "Wonderful, Papa!" I said, and was truly happy for him.

"We'll have a little money now."

I felt a surge of guilt about how I wasted money. The muddy shoes were probably ruined. Poor Papa worked so hard for all of us! He was always sending money to Grandma and Aunt Rosalie, who was unmarried, and Uncle Joe, who always managed to make a mess of finances. And he was always giving money away to friends and organizations, to almost anyone who asked.

As if to confirm my thoughts, Papa said, "I'm giving a thousand dollars to Mr. Neville for the Actor's Order."

"Papa! That's so generous! Too generous, maybe."

"No, daughter. Actors have not been well treated as a group in this society. No, in this case a thousand dollars is not too much." He made the slight dismissive gesture with his fingers that indicated that he considered a subject closed. "I assume Mr. Grossmann saw you safely to the party. How was it?"

"Very nice. I stayed rather late."

"Then you enjoyed yourself."

"I did." I went to the serving cart and fixed myself a plate of scrambled eggs and broiled fish and poured a cup of hot chocolate. When I was seated at the table, I decided to tell him about Downing. "I'm going to an exhibition this afternoon," I said. "Of the pyramids of Egypt."

"Very interesting."

"Yes. Downing Vaux is taking me."

He looked up from his letter. "Downing Vaux? Calvert's son? Julia's brother?"

I nodded. "Mr. McEntee's nephew. He's an artist also. Or he will be, soon."

"McEntee's spoken of him," he said thoughtfully. "He's older than you, isn't he?"

"Yes. He's in his late twenties."

"I don't think I know him."

"No, you don't. But you'll like him, Papa."

He smiled. "Well then, bring him around." He paused. "I wish I could join you for the exhibition. But I can't—we're rehearsing this afternoon. *Lear* is such a difficult play."

He returned to the letter he was reading. He did not even notice when a few minutes later I quietly stole out of the room.

When I went downstairs to meet Downing that afternoon, the lobby of the Brunswick was crowded, and I did not see him as I scanned the crowd for his thin form. I had almost decided he was late when I spotted him sitting stiffly in an armchair nearly hidden by an immense potted fern. As I approached him I saw that his face bore a strained expression, as though he were in pain. He was completely absorbed in his thoughts and did not see me even when I stood directly in front of him. "Mr. Vaux?"

"Oh, Miss Booth!" He abruptly stood up, inhaling sharply as though emerging from an underwater swim. "I didn't see you!"

"And I almost didn't see you, hidden over here by this plant. Mr. Vaux, are you well? You looked rather ill a moment ago."

"I'm quite well, thank you." He was tall, his pale face and light brown eyes well above my own. A high branch of the fern brushed against his neatly cut brown hair, mussing it.

I reached out and boldly linked my arm through his. "Shall we go? I'm quite excited about seeing these pyramids!"

He smiled down at me. "Miss Booth, I am so happy to see you! I so enjoyed our talk last night."

"I did also."

The fresh, cool air on the street was a welcome relief from the overheated lobby, and we both breathed deeply as we emerged.

The exhibition hall on Fourteenth Street was packed with a sluggishly moving crowd of well-dressed gentlemen and ladies, but in no time at all Downing had maneuvered us into a choice position before one of the main exhibits. "My father likes me to attend these exhibitions for inspiration," he whispered. "But the main thing I've learned from them is crowd navigation. Actually, I rather enjoy being part of a big crowd."

The exhibit consisted of several enlarged sepia photographs mounted in a triangular formation around an artist's rendering of a map of ancient Egypt. The photographs were of the Pyramids of Giza, taken from different angles. "They look so forbidding," I remarked.

"Yes, they do. Which is probably why the Egyptian style never caught on in this country, although it did enjoy some popularity back in the thirties. My father worked with it a little. It came to be used mainly in cemeteries. And of course our prison here in New York, the Tombs, is in that style."

"These are tombs, aren't they? For kings?"

"Yes. That one," he said, pointing to the Great Pyramid, "was built for a king named Cheops. It's the largest structure on earth."

"But it is more than that, young man!" said a small, fat man beside us. He stepped forward, and I saw that he resembled nothing so much as a storybook dwarf, with a long white beard and huge spectacles that greatly magnified his eyes. "Much more!"

He was speaking in a voice that was loud and a little too excited, not at all appropriate for a crowded public room. Embarrassed, Downing and I moved a bit closer to each other. People were starting to stare.

"One individual stands at the apex," he continued. "The

Creator sends the power to that individual, who then sends it to others. For the Egyptians, the pharaoh stood at the apex, but today the artist and the scientist do. Miss Booth, your father is one of those who stand there."

"Do I know you?" I asked, startled.

"No, you do not," he said, and rushed away from us by plowing directly into the crowd.

Downing scowled. "Who was that?"

"I don't know!"

When we'd seen enough of pyramids, we left and went to a nearby restaurant. It was quiet, not crowded, and softly lit by pink shaded lamps. The waiter showed us to a small table beside a window heavily draped with lace.

We ordered coffee and crumb cake. As we waited for it to arrive, Downing asked, "Did it disturb you to be singled out in that manner when we were viewing the pyramids?"

"Well, honestly, when someone is so strange—"

We both laughed. Then suddenly I heard myself say, "It only bothers me when they ask about John Wilkes Booth. I always say I don't remember."

Downing said nothing, but his change of expression showed how surprised he was that I'd said this. I myself could barely believe that I had. In my entire life I had never brought up The Subject of my own volition.

The waiter brought the coffee and cake. We sat silently while he placed it in front of us. Downing fingered a spoon. "Do you?" he asked gingerly after the waiter had left. "Do you remember anything?"

"I have a few memories of my uncle. I remember him rolling me on the floor and crawling under chairs with me. The only thing I remember about the assassination was understanding in a vague way that my father and all my relatives were terribly upset, and that Uncle John was the cause of it."

I took a small piece of the crumb cake. It tasted deliciously sweet, soft, and moist beneath a crumbly surface covered with powdered sugar. As I sat there comfortably with Downing, the subject of John Wilkes Booth seemed less forbidding than it ever had before. "I don't ordinarily speak about it," I told Downing. "You understand I can't talk to anyone in my family about this, and I've never felt comfortable enough with anyone else. But I do feel comfortable with you."

"You honor me, Miss Booth."

"I think it's that I trust you." I paused. "Things became very ugly, didn't they? I was too young to remember."

"Well, yes and no. It wasn't so bad here in New York, where there had never been as much support for Lincoln or the war as elsewhere in the North. Some terribly violent draft riots happened here. But in other parts of the North a great outcry against actors arose, because John Wilkes Booth was one. It was a difficult time for your family. Some of your relatives were jailed."

"My father?" I whispered.

"He fared better. He was in Boston, and the people there are civilized. Right away he came to New York. He issued a statement, an apology of sorts, also announcing his permanent retirement from the stage. I remember reading it in the newspapers. But my most vivid memory is of overhearing my parents discuss the despair he descended into. Apparently it all hit him very hard."

I thought of the one time I had seen the paralyzing black mood come over Papa, and knew it must have been the same, if not worse. I was glad I had so little memory of the things I was now hearing.

"The retirement lasted only half a year," Downing continued. "Requests for his return began to appear in the newspapers, especially the *Tribune*. And when he did reappear, he was welcomed back immediately. We were in the audience that night. There was a tremendous ovation when he appeared on the stage. Some people in the audience ran up and gave him flowers."

My eyes filled with tears. The public recognized that Papa gave them a great gift, wonderful art. Surely his great gift would more than compensate for the great wrong his brother had committed. Papa had almost immediately set about repaying the debt, plunging into his work even harder than before. Surely the accomplishments of Edwin would eventually eclipse the terrible action of John Wilkes, cancel the debt. Perhaps it was already canceled. People everywhere seemed to have nothing but the highest regard for Papa. Maybe people had already started to forget about John Wilkes Booth.

"Why did he do it?" I asked abruptly.

Downing sighed. "There's evidence that his first intention was only to kidnap Lincoln. He was distressed by the victory of the North. His support of the South was well known. He favored it as keenly as your father favored the North. But he didn't seem to understand that the South would have been better treated under Lincoln than under anyone else. It was widely known at the time that Lincoln favored leniency. Your uncle seems to have been confused." He glanced away from me. "Some people say he was more than confused. They say he was mad."

They say he was mad. The words echoed once, distantly, in my mind. What was madness? I thought again of Papa's black mood, and Mama's moods. Was that it? Or must it be something larger, more hideous?

I folded my hands in my lap and stared down at them.

Downing immediately apologized. "Please forgive me! I shouldn't have said that."

"No, no. Thank you for telling me. I'd rather learn it from you than in some other manner." I looked up and saw the genuine distress on his face. He must not be burdened with my troubles. Seeking to relieve him, I smiled.

His face cleared, and he smiled back at me.

That night I was waiting in the sitting room of the suite for Papa and Mama to return from the theatre. I fell asleep for a few minutes and had a bizarre little dream that Booth's Theatre was really a pyramid.

"We had a fine performance tonight, Edwina, simply wonderful!" cried Mama as they came in. "They gave us a standing ovation!" Then she coughed, a dry, rasping noise. When she had sufficiently recovered her breath, she said, "I think I'll take a hot, hot bath to drive out this New York cold." As the door to her room closed behind her I could only hope her coughing would prove to be no more than a New York cold. Her developing a serious physical illness in addition to her nervous problems could be devastating, for all of us.

"Edwina."

"Yes, Papa?'

"We'll be leaving for England in June."

Something in my throat tightened. "For how long, Papa?"

"Let's make it a vacation as well. A year, maybe longer."

I was glad the room was not brightly lit so he could not see the disappointment on my face. "How nice, Papa," I said in a constricted voice. "Good night."

From the next room came the muffled sounds of Mama coughing.

Back in my room, one question raced desperately through my mind: *Will Downing wait?* Pacing the floor, I wondered if he could possibly wait a whole year for me. I grabbed a lace handkerchief and twisted it mercilessly. I was nearly weeping with frustration. Perhaps I could stay behind when they went. But no, there was no reason for it. Were I engaged it might be possible, but not at this early stage of things. And besides, Papa needed me, especially with Mama not being well. No, my staying behind was out of the question. There was nothing for it; I would just have to go. I sobbed aloud, raising a hand to my forehead, and as I did so I caught sight of myself in the mirror over the dresser. I saw my stricken face, my reddened eyes, and the twisted handkerchief in my hands. Suddenly I felt very, very ashamed.

I sat down in an armchair and drew a deep breath. My train of thought changed, and I remembered that Downing Vaux was no impulsive young man. He would wait for me. A great surge of relief ran through me.

The trip now seemed more appealing. A year in Europe would greatly expand my knowledge, make me more Downing's equal, better equipped to assist him with his work. Yes, he would wait for me, and I would come back better than ever.

I was still thinking when Betty came in to help me get ready for bed. "Why are you just sitting there, missy?" she asked, peering down at me. "Something wrong?"

"No, everything's just fine." I smiled up at her. "We're going to Europe with Papa, Betty."

She groaned.

TWO

1881

Before we left America, Papa's friends told him to open in London in *Richelieu*. They counseled that Henry Irving, the current star there, was praised for his elaborate Shakespearean productions, and Papa should not appear to be imitating him. But during the trip across the Atlantic on the *Gallia* Mama insisted he could open in nothing but *Hamlet*. Unfortunately, her shrill voice prevailed. The opening-night audience at the Princess Theatre was cool, and the reviews the next morning were not good. A few of the critics thought Papa old-fashioned.

Although we knew the opening-night failure would be difficult to overcome, we were still managing to find some measure of enjoyment in the trip. Mama seemed especially pleased to be away from New York. Both her nervous condition and her physical health improved. Her rages and suspicions subsided, as did her tendency to cling to Papa, and her lingering cough almost completely vanished. It had been years since she had been so well, and Papa and I both marveled at the change in her. Even the bad reviews of the opening did not disturb her.

One evening that winter, on a night Papa was not performing, he, Mama, and I went to the Lyceum Theatre to see Mr. Irving perform. The idea was Mama's, to go quietly, without fanfare, to appraise "the competition" for ourselves. Three good orchestra seats were obtained for a performance of Tennyson's drama *The Cup*, currently viewed as Mr. Irving's latest triumph, in which he appeared with Ellen Terry. Miss Terry's acting talent, we had heard, was as vast as her beauty, and she was a great favorite of Londoners, who spoke of her as "our Ellen." Her relationship with Mr. Irving was strictly professional. There were people who said she had more talent in her little finger than Mr. Irving had in his entire being.

When the curtain rose we saw spectacular scenery and lighting, and exquisite costumes. Most stunning was the direction of the crowd scenes; Papa whispered that he had never seen a production in which they seemed so authentic. It was clear that Henry Irving was exceptionally talented, probably even a genius at stage design and direction. But when the man himself appeared onstage in the central role of Synorix, we saw within moments that his acting talent was not of the same caliber. His characterization of the role was extremely interesting and well presented. But at the center of his art lay intelligence rather than emotion. As an actor Henry Irving could interest an audience— intensely so—but he could never excite them. Realizing this, the three of us relaxed in relief.

A few minutes later Ellen Terry entered as Camma, the central female character. Her appearance brought to mind the ancient goddesses Juno and Demeter. Tall, statuesque, auburn-haired, Miss Terry was truly a great beauty, radiant with charm and charisma. While Mr. Irving was all intellect, she was all emotion, conveying an enormous array of feelings across the footlights with her every movement, word, and inflection. The audience, respectfully attentive while Mr. Irving was onstage, became charged with life each time she appeared. Papa leaned over and whispered, "She is obviously Irving's cash cow." I was shocked and a little dismayed to hear him make such a remark.

At the first intermission, one of Henry Irving's secretaries hurried down the aisle to where we were sitting. "Mr. Irving is honored to have you in the audience tonight, Mr. Booth," he said deferentially. "He would like to invite you to a small supper he is giving upstairs after the performance tonight."

"Will she be there?" Mama asked, her voice so low it was almost inaudible.

"Miss Terry? Yes. In fact, it was her idea to invite you."

A look of desperation flickered through Mama's eyes. Then her shoulders squared, and in a voice suddenly loud, she said grandly, "We will come!"

Papa and I exchanged glances. For the first time in months we heard a note of the old shrillness in her voice. "Perhaps we should rest tonight," I said carefully.

"No!" Mama's voice was so loud that several women in front of us turned and stared.

The secretary returned for us after the performance and escorted us upstairs to the supper. Mr. Irving greeted us with exquisite politeness, bowing formally to Papa and kissing my hand and Mama's. Tall, very thin, and elegant, he had a long, narrow face with a constant placid expression that told nothing of his thoughts. His movements were slow and fluid, and he wore academic-looking pince-nez spectacles. His voice, loud and clear onstage, in private sounded clipped and brittle, and his words were as guarded as his facial expression. He smiled blankly and uttered a crisp, simple "Thank you" when Papa praised his evening's work.

Mr. Irving beckoned a servant. "Shall we have champagne?" He turned to me. "Miss Booth? Some champagne?"

"Edwina's too young for that!" snapped Mama. "She'll get drunk!"

Mortified, I felt an overwhelming urge to turn and run from the room. But Mr. Irving asked in a gentle tone, "Some cider, then?" I nodded and, glancing at him, saw a fleeting look of compassion on his normally guarded face. He is kind, I thought, and intelligent. He understands all about us, and he has known us only a few minutes. I smiled at him, feeling better.

"Yes, cider, please, for all of us," said Papa.

Mama's eyes darted around the crowded room. "Where's Miss Terry?"

"She'll be here shortly," Mr. Irving replied.

"I used to act, you know," Mama abruptly told him.

"Oh?"

"I stopped when I married Mr. Booth. I felt it was more important to take care of him, and his daughter. Which hasn't been easy, let me say! Edwina requires my constant attention. I've practically raised her myself!"

I did not have time to respond to this fresh humiliation, for at that moment Ellen Terry appeared. Her entry into the room was as stunning as her earlier entry onstage. All eyes turned to her, and a momentary hush descended, punctuated by someone in the room sighing aloud, "Ellen!" She was wearing her costume from the final act of the play, a long, exotic dress of gold and silver silk. The flowers she had worn in her hair were still in place. With her, holding her hand, was a child, a boy about eight years old. He had an adorably plump face and a fine mop of golden hair.

Mama's eyes were riveted on the child. "Who's the little boy?" she asked Mr. Irving.

"That's her son, Teddy."

There was a silence before Mama said hoarsely, "I didn't know she had a child."

"Yes. She also has a little girl, slightly older."

All at once the grand manner Mama was using collapsed, as though some vital force inside her had suddenly given way, crumbled, or deflated. Her shoulders sagged, her hands drooped lifelessly to her sides, and her eyes became glassy and distant. She moved a little closer to Papa.

After settling her child with some friends, Ellen Terry came over to us. She smiled and apologized for being late. "But you see, my son turned up, and that caused me endless delay. How lovely to finally meet you!"

Papa complimented her performance. "Thank you kindly," she said with feeling. Strong and loud onstage, her voice was soft, full of gently shifting tones. "Have you ever done a Tennyson play? The words are beautiful, but it's rather difficult to put across. And the costumes for this play are almost impossible! Mr. Irving insists on accuracy wherever possible, you know."

"This one is lovely," I said.

She stared at me for a moment, apparently confused. Then she glanced down at her dress. Seeing what she had on, she gasped, raising a hand to her lips. "Oh, dear, this is what happens whenever Teddy turns up. I become hopelessly muddled!" She laughed musically and smoothed the front of her dress. "It *is* lovely, though, isn't it? Sometimes I think the nicest part of being an actress is all the wonderful costumes I'm allowed to wear." She tugged playfully on the skirt. "I'd never be allowed to wear this except on the stage."

The servant brought the cider, and some champagne for Miss Terry. Mr. Irving drank nothing. Other members of the Lyceum Company were introduced, and a little while later we sat down to supper. We were seated in places of honor near the head of the table. Although the mood was festive, Mama remained almost completely silent through the meal, responding to questions monosyllabically. Papa and I were both aware that there had been a dramatic shift in her mood, and we sought the earliest opportunity to leave.

When Mama excused herself to go to the powder room, I quickly followed. Mama finished first and went back out. A few minutes later I found her lingering in the dark corridor outside the room where the supper was being held. The entrance to the room was decorated with heavy red velvet draperies, and Mama was standing hidden behind one of them, peering in at the happy, laughing group. A fold of the velvet was clutched tightly in one hand.

I found it surprising that she had not gone in. "Mama," I said, but broke off when I realized she was trembling. A single tear glided down her cheek, and for the first time I understood she was very, very afraid. But of what, I did not know. I placed an arm protectively around her shoulder. "Come, Mama, this is no place for you," I said, and led her back into the brightly lit room.

At the table we found Papa engaged in conversation with Ellen Terry and her son. "I retired for a number of years to attend to my family," Miss Terry was telling Papa. "I returned to the stage only two years ago."

Ellen Terry was satisfied and accomplished both professionally and personally, bursting with creative vitality, at the peak of her popularity. She was everything Mama had once hoped to be. My arm around my stepmother's shoulder tightened.

That night Mama became wild over a trifle in her hotel room. Hours passed before Papa was able to calm her by administering a sedative drink, which she believed was poison. Finally she swallowed it, screeching, "Well, what of it! My life was ruined long ago!" She fell into a fitful sleep, and the next morning she was calmer, with no real memory of the night before. But her cough returned in full force, and a vaguely angry irrationality hovered about her. Mama's cough grew worse, her periods of mental lucidity grew shorter, and soon she was extremely ill.

After several eminent doctors had come to see her, she was finally diagnosed as having tuberculosis of the lungs and throat. The doctors were surprised she had lived so long with such a severe condition; indeed, she was so ill that she nearly died in Papa's dressing room at the theatre a few nights after the diagnosis. Her life depended upon her remaining in bed, the doctors told her, and so, for the first time in years, Papa performed without Mama hovering over him.

The Princess Theatre engagement ended in March. By that time, as I had expected after the disappointing opening-night reception, Papa's funds, professional reputation, and mood were all sagging. But then Henry Irving invited him to appear by his side in *Othello* at the Lyceum Theatre. The two stars would alternate in the roles of Othello and Iago, and Ellen Terry would play Desdemona. Papa was being offered the chance of a lifetime, making theatrical history before the curtain rose on the first performance.

While Papa was in rehearsal, Mama's parents, Sara and James McVicker, arrived in London. James McVicker was slow-moving, lugubrious, silent, and mentally dull. His inexpressive smooth pink face, framed by white whiskers and a receding hairline, was unlined, although he was well into his sixties. Sara was as lively as her husband was dull. Probably in her early fifties, she was small of stature, sprightly, and vivacious, with dark hair and eyes.

The McVickers began complaining the moment they

arrived—hardly what Papa needed while he prepared to appear with Mr. Irving. So I set about shielding him, placing myself as a buffer. When they complained, I placated them; when they criticized, I apologized. For the first time in my life I told lies. I had some twinges of conscience over them, but decided that lies told for a good cause were excusable. It was necessary to be a little ruthless in the service of great art.

Wisely, Papa cautioned me not to speak to Mama about his work, especially after *Othello* opened. But the McVickers told her everything, and even read portions of the splendid reviews to her. The fact that Papa could triumph without her was too much for her already troubled mind; it seemed to snap completely. "You dance on my grave!" she shrieked madly at Papa, accusing him of destroying her and cursing him so vehemently that I could hardly believe my ears. And then her mind would clear for a while and she would cling to him, weeping.

Othello at the Lyceum was a triumph for all concerned, including me. Practically overnight, Papa's popularity soared. Suddenly all the London newspapers were writing about the great tragedian from America; his old-fashioned style was forgotten. Theatres in France, Germany, and Italy all clamored for his appearance, offering small fortunes for a few nights' work. But instead of going on, riding the tide of popularity, he decided to turn around and go back to America. Mama was gravely ill, probably dying, and Papa thought it best to bring her home.

The necessity of our return caused me great disappointment on Papa's account. But I was also elated, for returning to America meant returning to Downing Vaux. I tried not to display this happiness in front of Papa, for I did not wish to hurt him by appearing insensitive to his disappointment. But I suspected he knew that I was happy to return, and why. He could not help but notice the many letters I had received from Downing during the many months of our absence.

Those letters, and the hopes of future happiness they represented, sustained me through those hard days in London. Contrary to my fears before leaving, Downing's interest in me had not waned but increased. His letters were intelligent, witty, concerned, interested, and, above all, frequent. They demonstrated one more way in which he was so exceptional, I thought with a thrill—that he so easily maintained a correspondence most people would find burdensome. For my part, the busier I became, the less time I had to write letters I considered worthy of his attention. But when I found time, I labored over each word with joy.

On June 30, 1881, nearly one year to the day after we had departed, the *Bothnia* steamed into New York harbor and docked. After most of the other passengers had disembarked, Papa and I came down the gangway with Mama supported between us. Her parents followed several yards behind.

Reporters from the various newspapers were clustered near the foot of the gangway. Seeing Papa, they immediately rushed toward us. Mama cried out in fear. Her entire body trembled as she hid her face against Papa's chest.

"Gentlemen, please," Papa said quietly. The reporters, understanding the gravity of Mama's condition, respectfully backed off a few feet.

"He'll take questions tomorrow," I told them, smiling wanly. "We'll be at the Brunswick Hotel." The reporters stepped aside, and the three of us went into the customs house. The McVickers lingered outside a while before following us in.

Papa had wired the Brunswick in advance to reserve rooms

for all of us, including the McVickers. Two suites had been reserved, including Papa's usual one, but the McVickers insisted on being close to Mama, so I occupied the room previously used by her. Although the room was quite large and crowded with good furniture, the color scheme was a gloomy green, and the single window filled it with a constant glare of hard northern light. The white marble fireplace, unused now in summer, had the look of a tombstone. I would have vastly preferred being back in my cheerful sunny room across the hall. However, the new arrangement had one distinct advantage: we were away from the McVickers.

Whatever small doubts about the depth of Downing's interest I still had when we arrived in New York were dispelled when I entered the suite at the Brunswick. There, waiting for me on the table, was a large bouquet of white roses, with a simple card from Downing saying he would call on me the next day.

"The roses are from Mr. Vaux," I told Papa, trying not to sound too pleased and excited. Papa had come in with me, and had heard my gasp of delight upon seeing the bouquet.

"They are in perfect bloom," he said quietly. "Well, I must meet this young man."

"Tomorrow, Papa. He's coming tomorrow, and you'll meet him then." Suddenly I was worried that I sounded too anxious. "Unless that's too soon?"

Papa laughed. "It appears he's already coming. No, tomorrow is fine."

Late the next morning Papa was interviewed by a large group of reporters from the New York newspapers in one of the main-floor parlors of the Brunswick. I sat formally by his side on a fashionably uncomfortable horsehair sofa as he answered a host of questions about his London engagement. Topics ranging from the talent of Henry Irving to the quality of service in London hotels were presented for his comments, all of which were rapidly scribbled down.

Toward the end of the session, one of the reporters asked bluntly, "How's Mrs. Booth's health?"

The pause before Papa replied was nearly undetectable. "Mrs. Booth has been ill for several years, gentlemen." Beside him, I nodded gravely.

From the back of the group a nasal voice rang out: "Is it true you refused to take her to southern France when the doctors recommended it for her health?"

I gasped aloud. But without missing a beat, Papa said flatly, "No."

"Sir, would you care to comment on the story about your trip that appeared in this morning's *Dramatic News*?"

"I haven't seen it," he said calmly, "but since this is the first time I've spoken on the subject, I doubt it can be very accurate." He stood up, took my hand, and drew me to my feet. "Now, gentlemen, as you may imagine, I have much to attend to. Thank you for your continuing interest in my career." He led me from the room.

Not until the door of our suite closed behind us did I realize I was holding my entire body tense, as though I were in danger of being physically attacked. But we *had* just been attacked, I thought as my muscles relaxed. The reporters had tried to catch us off guard about Mama's illness by baiting us with a lie. But Papa had not allowed himself to be trapped. Foolish little men, thinking they could do that to Edwin Booth!

"Where do you think they heard that awful lie about refusing to take Mama to France?" I asked Papa.

"Reporters are frequently misinformed."

"What do you think is in the *Dramatic News?*"

"Unfortunately, I suspect it's something about Mary's illness. That was what the sequence of questions suggested."

"Why should it concern them?" I said angrily. "They ought to concentrate on all the important things you do. How many truly great actors are there in America? Perhaps you ought not give any interviews until they show more intelligence and respect!"

"And where would we be then?" Papa's voice was unusually cold and stern. "Where would my career be were the press to lose interest in me? I can assure you, shortly afterward the public as well would lose interest."

"But, Papa, doesn't it infuriate you when they tell blatant lies and pry into your personal life?"

"Of course it does. Regrettably, it sometimes occurs. However, it is vastly preferable to have their interest with those unpleasant aspects than not to have it at all. One in my position must always treat the press with respect, Edwina. Our livelihood depends on it, to a great degree." Then in a softer tone he added, "Many years ago I learned that even the most wretched occurrence in your personal life cannot harm you if your work is truly good. If the truth cannot harm you, how can silly lies? No, never fear the interest of the press or the public, even if it at times seems irrelevant. Fear only their lack of interest."

My indignation crumbled as his words settled in my mind. He was right. An artist with a creative message was not much good if no one received the message. A little personal privacy was a small sacrifice. Sheepishly I looked at the floor. "Papa, I'm sorry I'm so slow in understanding these things. I do want to be a help to you."

"My life has not been easy, daughter. But having you has always made it easier."

I had sent Downing a note asking him to come by at two o'clock. Precisely at two the bell on the hotel telephone in the parlor rang, and the front-desk clerk informed me that Mr. Vaux had arrived and was on his way up. I glanced nervously at myself in the mirror over the fireplace. To Betty's dismay, I had changed my dress three times before settling on the demure, conservative gray-and-white cotton afternoon dress I now had on. Seeing my final choice, Betty had grown silent. Then she grumbled, "You're the strange one, missy. That dress makes you look ten years older."

"I want to look sensible."

"Sensible ladies don't change their dresses three times before going out."

The somber cotton dress did little, however, to suppress my excitement when Downing entered the suite. As he came in I studied him as carefully as possible without appearing to stare. Aside from being a little thinner, his face more angular, he looked exactly the same as he had a year before. I found my ability to detect these small changes comforting and reassuring. There had been times over the past year when, for all my deepening interest, I experienced the odd sensation of not being able to remember precisely how he looked.

Papa remained seated in the armchair by the fireplace until I brought Downing in to him. He rose and cordially extended his hand. Downing took it and shook it gently. I noticed he was half a head taller than Papa.

"I met you when you were a child," said Papa, sitting back down.

"Papa, you didn't tell me that!" I sat down with Downing

on the sofa, facing Papa. That he had not mentioned this before disturbed me. Suddenly I was gripped with fear as for the first time it occurred to me that he might dislike Downing. A lump of ice seemed to form in my chest. Why hadn't I thought of this before? I wondered with mounting anxiety. And if he doesn't like him, what happens then? I stared at Papa's face, although I knew it was a useless thing to do. Years ago I learned you could never tell his reaction to people from his face.

"It was long ago," Papa said placidly to me. "Before you were born."

Downing looked puzzled. "What was the occasion, sir?"

"A few of us were visiting your uncle Jervis at his studio. Your father stopped by with you. Jervis asked you to paint something for us."

"Not that time!" Downing rolled his eyes. "You were there?"

Papa nodded. "I remember it well. You, apparently, did not wish to paint for us. But then your father spoke sharply to you, and you sat down and painted a little picture that was very nice indeed."

Downing again looked puzzled. He started to say something, but stopped. Instead, he smiled and folded his hands in his lap.

"What an obedient little boy, I thought to myself," said Papa.

I laughed nervously. "Papa remembers so many little things," I said to Downing.

"Edwina tells me you're an artist," Papa said.

"I aspire to be one. It will be some time before I'm ready to paint. Now, most of the time I assist my father, taking care of many of the commercial details of his work for him. Meeting with tradesmen, purchasing materials, and such. It allows him to concentrate on his designs."

Just as I've been helping Papa, I thought. Papa would appreciate that. As if in answer to my thoughts, Papa said, "Well then, you must be invaluable to him."

"I like helping him," Downing replied. Grinning boyishly, he added, "The great advantage is that I can take time off whenever I choose. My father is adamant about having nothing obstruct my development as an artist. Too often, he says, artists are prevented from developing by the pressure to earn a living. He says he has always sworn that no child of his would ever feel that pressure. I do understand how fortunate I am in this. Few artists have such an opportunity."

"You are fortunate," said Papa.

"What my father does not understand, though, is that I like helping him. I don't find the things I do for him to be drudgery."

The conversation paused. Then, with enormous relief, I heard Papa say, "Your father must be very proud of you. I can see why Edwina thinks so highly of you."

We chatted pleasantly for a few more minutes. Then Papa stood up. "I mustn't keep you from your walk in the park."

A crease formed between Downing's eyebrows. "Is that what you'd like to do?" he asked me.

"If you'd like to. I hadn't decided."

"I'm sorry," interrupted Papa. "For some reason I thought that was your plan for this afternoon, perhaps because the weather is so beautiful. It seems a shame not to take advantage of it."

"It *is* a nice afternoon," I said. "The park would be refreshing."

"Then we'll go," said Downing, standing up. I fetched my handbag and parasol, I kissed Papa good-bye, and we left.

Our carriage was traveling up Broadway toward Central Park when Downing said, "That wasn't what happened, you know. The time your father spoke of."

"About meeting you when you were little?"

"Yes. He was right up to a point, about my not wanting to paint. But the outcome was very different. I didn't paint anything. After my father scolded me, I became very angry and smeared the paints all over everything, including my clothes. My father was furious, and we left at once."

I laughed. "Papa's version is much more flattering to you."

"True."

"Do you remember why you didn't want to paint?"

"I remember very well. Uncle Jervis kept a great box filled with pennies, and he always let me play with them when I visited. I loved to make little piles and play at being a banker. I was happy when I learned we would stop by that day, since then I could play with the pennies. But they wouldn't let me; they wanted me to paint. I was so angry, I decided I would not do as they wished."

"And you didn't."

"I didn't. But you see, I didn't get to do what I wanted to do, either. I should have complied with their wishes and painted something, and then maybe there would have been time left for me to play with the pennies." He leaned back in the seat. "I believe I learned something very important from that incident."

"What was that?"

"Life requires cooperation."

"Yes," I agreed. "Some sacrifices tend to be necessary to get what is really important."

"So it seems."

"It's strange, though, that Papa doesn't remember what really happened. His memory is usually excellent."

"I made such a mess, I don't know how anyone could forget it." Downing hesitated a moment, then added, "When your father was telling me about it, I had the oddest sensation that he knew very well it had been otherwise."

"Perhaps he did. Perhaps he wished to spare you embarrassment. Yes, I'm sure that's it. Papa's that way about hurting people's feelings."

"He's a gentleman."

"He liked you very much. But I knew he would."

"I'm glad, Miss Booth. Very glad."

The carriage stopped near Sixtieth Street, near the southern end of the park, and we got out and entered the park for our walk.

Papa had the *Dramatic News* waiting for me when I returned. The story the reporters mentioned was on the second page.

Edwin Booth has in recent months completely neglected the health of his wife, with the result that Mrs. Booth is now dangerously ill. An informed source reports that Mr. Booth insisted she remain with him in London while he performed long after her doctors advised her removal to a warmer climate. At times he even insisted upon her accompanying him to the theatre …

"This is outrageous!" I cried, angrily throwing the paper down. "It's all turned around. Anyone who knows us knows it was Mama who insisted on staying near you in the dressing room!"

"Yes. The people who matter to us know the truth already and will recognize this for what it is. It troubles me not at all. The only aspect that troubles me is your being upset by it."

Immediately I composed myself. Now I had disturbed him again, twice in one day over the same thing. That was almost as bad as Mama! I would have to learn to control myself better. In a cool voice I said, "I'm not upset, Papa dear. You needn't worry about me at all."

Later, Betty said to me, "I peeked out and saw your Mr. Vaux this afternoon. He's older than you, isn't he?"

"About ten years. That's not too much."

"Too much for what?"

"Oh, companionship," I said evasively.

"Has he been sick?"

"No. What a curious thing to think! Why do you ask?"

"He looked a little washed out."

"Oh, honestly, Betty! You're being silly."

She shrugged. "I hope so, missy."

The next morning Papa and I went in to see Mama. The return to America had improved her health, and we found her sitting up in bed playing cards with her mother. Throughout her illness she had considered her appearance to be of paramount importance, and she now used her small rally of strength to improve it. She was still confined to bed, but her hair had been curled and braided in an attractive new coiffure, her face powdered and rouged, her fingernails polished. Pearl earrings were clipped to her ears, and she wore a striking Oriental-style bed jacket of red silk, intricately embroidered with jet-black onyx and tiny seed pearls. But the curls, powder, and rouge did little to conceal the wasted, skull-like quality of the face beneath, and the jewelry and pretty garments could not hide the mortally ill body.

The room was hot, the window tightly shut to keep the slightest breeze from reaching Mama and chilling her. The heavy scent of perfume in the air could not mask the unmistakable odor of a sickroom.

"So you finally found your way here," she said sullenly as we came in. Her voice was little more than a hoarse rasping sound. Mrs. McVicker looked up from her seat next to the bed. She produced the faintest of smiles, then gathered up the cards from her daughter's lap and proceeded to shuffle them.

Papa went to the bed, bent down, and kissed Mama's sunken cheek. "You're looking well today, Mary."

"I'll be up and about in no time," she croaked.

I came forward. "Hello, Mama," I said, bending down to kiss her. As I did so, the collar of her bed jacket parted a little and revealed a strand of perfectly matched pearls that I recognized as my own. They had belonged to my mother, and Papa had given them to me on my fifteenth birthday. Months ago I had loaned them to Mama when she admired them, and she had never returned them. I cared little for jewelry, and under other circumstances would have been inclined to let her keep them. But these had belonged to my mother, and I wanted them. I would ask Papa to get them back for me.

"What a lovely jacket, Mama," I said, standing up.

"Isn't it? Father bought it for me yesterday."

"James thought a little gift might cheer her spirits," Mrs. McVicker said, without looking up. "He is so very busy, but still he found time." She stopped shuffling and dealt out the cards, making a pile for herself and one for her daughter.

Papa pulled two chairs up on the other side of the bed, and we sat down. A vast array of medicine bottles lined the bedside table, all different sizes and shapes and colors. I wondered if their contents were keeping Mama alive.

Mama picked up her cards and stared at them without

much interest. "Another rotten hand," she muttered. Then she suddenly looked up at Papa. "Edwin, I've been thinking. As soon as I'm better I want to start acting with you again. We could begin this fall. What are our plans? Do we tour?"

I looked at the medicine bottles and held back a little sob. She couldn't accept it that she was dying, I thought sadly.

"Nothing's definite, Mary," Papa said.

"And do you know what play I want to do? *The Cup*. The one we saw Henry Irving and Ellen Terry do in London. We'll do it the way it should be done! We could tour all over America and then take it to England. Maybe we could even do it at the Lyceum—" She stopped abruptly, staring off into the distance beyond his head. Then in a dull voice she added, "But you've already acted there."

Mrs. McVicker glared at Papa, as though blaming him for agitating Mama. "Your cards, dear," she said to her daughter.

Mama looked down at the cards she was holding and squinted as if she didn't recognize them. Then she glanced around suspiciously. "These aren't my cards," she said slowly. "Someone's changed them when I wasn't looking. I had better ones than these!" She looked accusingly at me.

Mrs. McVicker said nothing; she did not even look up. Mama was starting to breathe rapidly, which always brought on a coughing fit. Deftly, Papa reached out and took the cards from her. "Well, Mary, your mother's an honest woman. I'm sure she won't mind reshuffling."

Mrs. McVicker stared at him with hate in her eyes. "Give them to me!" she snapped, and reached out and snatched the cards from his hand.

"This time, Mary, I'll watch and make sure no one touches them," said Papa.

"So will I," said Mrs. McVicker, shuffling violently.

Papa and I stayed a while longer, until Mama seemed to grow tired. On the way out we encountered Mr. McVicker in the parlor of the suite. Startled at the sight of us, he shuffled some newspapers he was carrying.

"I'm arranging for a new doctor to see her," Papa told him. Then he glanced at the newspapers. "Terrible slander in the *Dramatic News.*"

Mr. McVicker nodded and looked away. He then presented Papa with a sheath of bills to be paid, Mama's expenses.

Back in our suite, I asked, "Why did you mention that horrible story to him?"

"To stop it."

I stared at him. "You think he's the source?"

"Of course."

"Papa, Mama had on my pearls, the ones that were my mother's. I lent them to her and she never returned them. Can you get them back?"

"I'll try."

Papa glanced over the bills Mr. McVicker had given him for payment. Then, smiling wryly, he showed me the bill for Mama's new red bed jacket, included with the rest.

On our third day back in America, July 2, 1881, President Garfield was shot by an insane man named Charles Guiteau. Although the shooting happened in a Washington railroad station, it affected us as if it had taken place in our New York City hotel suite. Almost at once everyone had an insatiable interest in assassins. Stories about John Wilkes Booth appeared in all the leading newspapers, soon followed by other tales of the Booth family.

"People were starting to forget," I said bitterly to Downing when he visited me at the hotel.

"Pay it no mind."

"If it's this dreadful now, I can imagine how bad it was then." For the first time in my life I felt anger toward my dead uncle. The pain he caused his family was nearly unforgivable. "My poor father. It's amazing he was able to continue."

"What does he say about all this now?"

"Nothing. I pretend I don't read the newspapers. It's easier for him if he thinks I don't know about it. Besides, most of it's too disgusting to talk about." I laughed nervously. "What could I say to him? 'Papa, is it true your brother was mad? Or was it simply his drunkenness?'" I laughed again, more harshly this time.

Embarrassed, Downing cleared his throat.

"I'm sorry," I said. "Please forgive me."

"These stories are vicious."

"And have you seen all the lies about how Papa mistreated my stepmother?" Several more stories had appeared in the *Dramatic News*. Charles Guiteau had created the perfect atmosphere for the McVickers' lies to flourish in, I thought with a bitterness for which I immediately felt guilty.

"Ignore them," said Downing. "Intelligent people pay no attention to all that nonsense. Only the worst people are interested in it."

"Someday they'll forget," I said resolutely. "Someday no one will remember John Wilkes Booth."

Julia arrived, loaded down with boxes from a morning spent shopping on the nearby Ladies Mile. I had intended to accompany her, but with everything in the newspapers I had changed my mind and instead asked her to join her brother and me in the suite for lunch. I was in no mood to be stared at.

When we were finished, Downing left to return to his father's office.

"Edwina, he's so relaxed with you," Julia commented to me. "How do you manage it?"

"It has nothing to do with me. He's such a kind person. And so intelligent! He knows so much about everything."

"He's learned much from my father." Pride filled her voice. "From when he was a little boy, my father has been teaching him, especially about art and architecture. He wants him well prepared to make his way in the world. But, Edwina—" She hesitated.

"What is it, Julia?"

"Please, you must never repeat this."

"Never."

"I don't think Downing is going to do the same type of work as my father."

"Will your father be hurt?"

"No. He has always said that if Downing displayed some greater artistic talent he would encourage him to develop it." She paused. "He cares only that he doesn't waste his life in some meaningless work. He's very proud of Downing's painting, and he encourages it. I think he hopes that one day Downing will be an accomplished artist."

"I am sure he will be. Yes, I am sure of it." Without a doubt Downing had a great artistic gift, a gift I could possibly assist in delivering.

"She could linger for years in her present condition. But you must understand she will never recover, not at this late stage."

The new doctor Papa had brought in had just finished his examination of Mama. Papa and I sat silently in the parlor of our suite as we listened to his report. The doctor was a highly recommended specialist in tubercular illnesses. He was a handsome, middle-aged man with an air of crisp directness about him.

"She will not recover," he repeated briskly. "You do understand that?"

"Yes," said Papa. This was no surprise. In London the doctors had been clear about the fatal nature of her disease.

"I stress this because she obviously believes otherwise. I was fairly sure it was a delusion caused by her mental disorder, but I felt it best to ask just to be certain."

"I'm considering a sanitarium," said Papa. "Do you recommend it?"

The doctor hesitated, but only briefly. "Sir, I'll be completely honest. I'd advise a sanitarium if I thought it would help. But it won't. They're very expensive, and you'd simply be wasting your money. I detest putting it this way, but it really doesn't matter where she is from now on, so long as her needs are met. And from what you tell me, she's frequently unaware of where she is anyway."

"Doctor, in the fall I must continue my work, which entails travel. Will my departure have a negative effect?"

"Does your presence calm her?"

"No. In fact, quite the contrary, as her parents frequently tell me."

"Then there's no reason for you to remain, once you're certain she's well cared for. Remember, though, the end could come at any time. You don't want to be too far away."

Long Branch was a popular seaside community near the northern tip of the New Jersey coast. Uncle Joe, Papa's youngest brother, maintained a permanent residence there, and Papa's mother and his sister Rosalie lived with him. Their home on Ocean Avenue was a large, rambling Queen Anne–style house. It had many rooms, so I was easily accommodated when Papa brought me there for the remainder of the summer.

Despite the presence of three of my relatives and twice as many servants, I soon found myself feeling bored and lonely. Papa was not there for me to look after, having departed to visit friends in Connecticut. Betty spent most of each day with the other servants in the lower regions of the house. Grandma Booth was good company, for she was always pleasant, never cross or irritable, but she was getting on in years and spent most of the day sleeping or resting in her bedroom. I hardly ever saw Uncle Joe, who was busy with his real estate transactions and kept to himself most of the time. Aunt Rosalie was more visible, but she seldom spoke. I had learned years ago not to attempt to draw her into conversation, which she seemed to dislike. Whenever I encountered her, sitting next to the stained-glass window in the parlor with her sewing box or drifting through one of the many upstairs hallways, she would smile kindly at me but not say a word. Aunt Rosalie spoke only if questioned directly or on matters of urgency.

The day after I arrived, I walked to a local shop to purchase some thread for Aunt Rosalie. The clerk at the counter was engaged in a lively discussion of the President with a customer. They grew quiet when they saw me, and I was sure they stared as I left. The next day I visited a pair of sisters in the neighborhood with whom I had become friendly on earlier visits. They were delighted to see me, and we chatted happily about all sorts of things. Before long one of them plunged into the subject of Garfield and Guiteau. Her sister turned rigid and stared at her, which stopped the discussion but cast an embarrassed feeling over the remainder of the visit. The following day, in the town library, I saw a prominently displayed notice of an upcoming lecture entitled "Great Assassins and Assassinations in History." After this, I decided I preferred to use my time in Long Branch for rest and relaxation, as I wrote to Papa, "not for tiring socializing."

Social activities for young people in Long Branch were bountiful, and in the past I had joined in. But this summer I was reluctant to do so. President Garfield had for many years owned a summer house in the southern part of Long Branch, and he was known personally by many of the residents. Because of this, interest in his condition was even keener in Long Branch than it had been in New York. His condition, and what had brought him to it, was on everyone's lips. Naturally reclusive, my other relatives appeared unaware of this, but I found out soon after my arrival.

Although I spoke to Downing of these distressing incidents at first, I was eventually less inclined to do so. He never brought any of it up himself. Initially I thought this was due to politeness and concern for my feelings, for I knew he read several newspapers daily and must have seen all the stories. Then I discovered he was oblivious to it all; he simply didn't care. This was a great relief to me, for I had a hazy fear that it might cause his feelings for me to change. When I discovered he never thought about it, I counted myself fortunate and thereafter saw no reason to direct his thoughts to it. I must never distract him with unrelated problems of my own, especially not with this specific problem from the past. It must never be allowed to interfere with another artist's peace of mind the way it had interfered with Papa's.

Long Branch was only a few hours from New York by train or steamer, and Downing made several trips to see me. These were the few occasions on which I would leave the house, usually for long walks on the beach. Downing did not seem to notice that I always steered clear of any place where we were likely to encounter many people.

"I thought you might find the ocean views inspiring," I remarked on one of these walks.

He shrugged. "To me it just looks empty. Sky, water, and nothing else."

I did not agree, for I had always been charmed by the shifting play of light on the cresting and breaking waves. I simply decided Downing would not be a marine artist, in the same way that Papa was not a comic actor. Thereafter, we began to spend our time in the enclosed garden behind the house.

Julia visited me once during the summer. Unlike her brother, she was very surprised when I did not wish to go to the Ocean Hotel or one of the other fashionable places for lunch. When she further learned that I had no desire to go bathing in the ocean, she was confused.

"But isn't that why people come to Long Branch? To go in the ocean?"

"Well, some people. I haven't been in the water once the entire summer. I don't even have a bathing outfit."

"We can rent them on the beach."

I sighed. "Julia dear, I just don't feel I want to be around a crowd of people so much this summer." I considered bringing up The Subject but decided against it. Instead, I told her it was simply not a very happy time for me, "with my stepmother so ill, and all the trouble that's caused."

She patted my hand. "Of course. I understand."

We spent most of the afternoon in the garden playing dominoes, her favorite game. At one point while we were chatting she arranged the little tiles upright in a long row and then casually pushed over the one at the end, causing the entire line to topple.

But instead of laughing I found myself imagining that the first tile had been my uncle John.

During the summer any guests we had from New York came and went by steamer, which was the fastest way between there and Long Branch. Although uncomfortable with the crowd, I always went to the Ocean Pier to greet them when they arrived and to see them off when they left.

On one occasion when Downing was leaving we arrived to find a small crowd gathered around the gangplank. Downing, able to see the cause of it, reported, "It's General Grant and his wife. They seem to be leaving for New York."

I swallowed dryly. I had forgotten that General Grant, the former president, also owned a summer cottage in Long Branch. In light of recent events, this was an unpleasantly significant realization. One of the few things I did know about the assassination of President Lincoln was that General and Mrs. Grant had initially planned to sit with the Lincolns in their box at Ford's Theatre that fateful night.

"The Grants just bought a townhouse in New York, you know," Downing said casually. "They'll be living there permanently from now on."

I was not comforted by the idea of the Grants living in New York. I had lately come to think of New York City as my home, where I had made friends since finishing school. All summer I looked forward to returning there, where the notoriety to my family caused by the Garfield situation was less severe. But now the Grant family would be there! They had sons my age, whom I would undoubtedly encounter socially, and every time I did people would think of that night at Ford's Theatre.

Eventually it would all die down, though, I reasoned. In the meantime I would be going with Papa on a lengthy tour of the Southern states in the fall. By the time we returned, people would have largely forgotten all this unpleasantness.

Downing boarded the steamer, and I tried to remain inconspicuous in the rear of the crowd through the torturous moments until it departed. Finally it started off, and with steady self-discipline I waved good-bye to Downing, remaining until the crowd began to disperse. Then, as I started to leave, I saw two elderly women staring at me. One of them turned and whispered into the ear of the other, and I knew that once again I had been identified as the niece of John Wilkes Booth.

Papa was scheduled to open at Booth's Theatre on October 3, and early in September we returned to New York for his rehearsals. At first we planned on taking rooms at a new hotel, the Windsor. But Mr. McVicker notified Papa that he was moving Mama to a house he had rented on West Fifty-fourth Street, so we returned to our familiar suite at the Brunswick.

Throughout the summer Papa continued to pay Mama's bills, and in return received periodic but brief accounts of her condition. This news he would pass along to me in his letters. According to the McWickeds, as Papa now frequently called them, Mama had stabilized once Papa left, and continued to do nicely in his absence. The unspoken message was clear: Papa should stay away.

This arrangement suited me fine. Papa's superb performance with Mr. Irving in London had shown the true heights he was capable of reaching when free of distractions. I thought of this often during the summer and came to have strong feelings about the way Mama impeded Papa's career. I was amazed he had been able to create at all under such trying circumstances. The current separation was not a bad idea.

Over the past year, much of the anger I felt toward Mama had been tempered by equal feelings of pity and concern. No matter how bitter or stinging my grievances prior to my entering her sickroom, they were always lessened when I emerged, replaced by feelings of empathy and sadness. This was even the case when Mama behaved unpleasantly. Only later, when I had time to think, did the bitterness and resentment come creeping back. During the summer in Long Branch I had a long time to think, and brood, and there were no sobering visits to Mama to curb these thoughts. By the time I returned to New York with Papa, I had built up a mountain of anger toward Mama.

On September 19 President Garfield died. For a few days a surge of interest in assassins filled the papers; then it sharply declined. Now, only the upcoming trial of Charles Guiteau remained before it would be finished.

Near the end of September Papa told me he had written to Mama, inquiring if she would like him to visit her. "A conciliation before the end comes would be for the best," he told me. Although I felt this was a mistake, I bit my tongue and said nothing. When Mama's response came back that she would see Papa only if he would admit in writing that he had behaved terribly to both her and her parents, I could barely contain my rage. Then I remembered my pearls.

There had been no opportunity for Papa to get them back, and they had gone with Mama to the house on West Fifty-fourth Street. Under the current circumstances there was little hope of their being returned, and I had to admit they were probably gone forever. I clenched my fists in frustration. The pearls were mine, and I wanted them. They had been my real mother's. I was outraged to think that Mama could deprive me of them!

Suddenly I was seized with determination to get them back.

I sat down and waited calmly until Papa left for rehearsal. Then I went to his correspondence, took out the letter from Mama, and copied down the address.

An hour later I stood in front of the house on West Fifty-fourth Street. One in a row of brownstones, it looked the same as others I'd been inside many times. Once inside I would have little difficulty locating Mama's bedroom and finding her jewelry box. I took a deep breath, glided up the front steps, and tried the handle of the front door. Luck was with me; it was unlocked. I slipped into the front hallway.

The heavy wooden doors to the drawing room were closed, and the staircase ahead was thickly carpeted. I wasted no time but hurried directly toward the stairs. As I passed the drawing room I heard the sounds of female voices engaged in conversation. A distant, shrill note of laughter rang out. I was certain it came from Mama. She was certainly doing well if she was up and receiving guests at an afternoon tea, I thought bitterly.

Upstairs, the overpowering smell of perfume led me to Mama's door. As soon as I opened it I saw that the entire room was swathed in white lace, as though a giant spider had been at work for years. Long, spreading draperies covered the windows, lace tablecloths and doilies were spread over the tables, and lacy antimacassars were on the chairs. Near one wall was a large canopied bed, adorned with curtains of lace and frothy, silvery chiffon. But for all the wealth that had been lavished on its decorations, the room was not well kept. The bed was unmade, a frilly jumble of pillows and blankets in its center. No fresh air had entered the room in a long while, and the smells of medicine and sickness were clearly detectable beneath the perfume.

I went straight to the vanity table. Amidst a plethora of perfumes, powders, rouges, and medicine bottles sat Mama's large jewelry box. I was just reaching to open it when a thin, feeble voice, barely more than a whisper, called out weakly behind me, "Please, a drink of water ..."

Startled, I turned around, expecting to find that someone had come in behind me, but there was no one. "Please, water," came the voice again, and something stirred in the pile of pillows and coverings on the bed. Slowly I went to it and looked down.

Sunken into the pillows and blankets lay Mama, her body shriveled. She seemed to be only partly conscious. Her breathing was labored, her throat contracting with each shallow breath. Her skin, dried and yellow, barely contained the bones beneath, which threatened to burst through at any moment. Her swollen eyes bulged beneath their closed eyelids, and her hair was a tangled brittle mass on the pillow. Aghast, I could only stare at the corpse-like body surrounded by the frilly, lacy pillows. It seemed as though a fly was withering and dying in the folds of a great web in which it had become entangled.

"Water," whispered Mama again, this time almost inaudibly. Numbly I responded, looking around until I saw a pitcher and glass on the bedside table. With trembling hands I half filled the glass and held it to Mama's cracked lips. She weakly took a few sips, then moved her head a tiny bit to indicate she was done. "Thank you, nurse," she whispered as the glass was removed.

Tears came to my eyes. Here was Mama, in great pain and clearly close to death, remembering her manners. "A lady must always be polite, no matter the circumstances," she had once told me. "It's Edwina, Mama," I whispered.

Mama should never have been left alone in this condition. The chatter and laughter of the women downstairs carried through the house. An anger close to rage swept over me.

Mama was lying here, mortally ill, calling for water, while her mother was downstairs with friends, laughing and chattering! Why, it was hideous, revolting!

I looked down at the ravaged body on the bed. The mind within was as badly damaged, if not more so. A great sense of grief and remorse came over me. I had actually begun to hate her, I thought dully. With terrible shame and guilt I realized that for the past months I had been waiting for her death. Waiting, and hoping for it to come soon.

I sobbed aloud. How could I have done that? Hated her, wished her dead? This was Mama! Mama, who had read me bedtime stories, heard my prayers, and bought me dolls. Mama, who taught me how to be a lady, how to choose the right clothes, and how to dance!

Later, I couldn't remember leaving Mama's bedroom and getting out to the street, or if I encountered anyone in the process. The next thing I knew, I was climbing into a carriage at the corner of Fifty-fourth and Broadway. "Good-bye, Mama," I whispered to the air as the carriage started toward Madison Square. I had forgotten all about my pearls.

My engagement to Downing Vaux was announced on October 2. The wedding, however, was not to take place for at least a year. The delay was a disappointment to Downing, but everyone else felt it was best. Downing's parents wanted him to have another year free before assuming the responsibilities of marriage. Papa felt that another year of exposure to the world would better prepare me for married life. For me, the most important reason for waiting was that I planned to accompany Papa on his tour of the South and East for most of the coming year. The tour, again managed by Mr. Abbey, was to be unusually long and extensive, with overnight stops in many places. It would be exhausting for Papa. And he would need my help through the ordeal of Mama's death, more imminent than Papa knew. For reasons I did not fully understand, I said nothing to him or anyone else about my visit to the house on West Fifty-fourth Street. The upcoming year, with its personal and professional trials, was not the time for Papa to adjust to being alone. I was satisfied to wait until the following summer to set a date for the wedding.

The day after the engagement was announced, Papa's tour began at Booth's Theatre with Shakespeare's *Othello*. Papa played the role of the evil Iago. *Macbeth* had originally been scheduled, but a play with a political assassination as its subject matter was not appropriate to perform so soon after President Garfield's death. *Othello*, a tale of jealousy and deceit, was deemed more suitable. Besides, news of Papa's triumph in the play with Mr. Irving the previous season in London had traveled back to America, and Mr. Abbey knew the public would be interested.

I attended the first matinee performance after the opening. Downing had intended to accompany me but at the last minute had been prevented by a small emergency over some materials ordered by his father, so I found myself alone in the special box at Booth's Theatre reserved for the star's family. It was the same box I had sat in with Julia more than a year before for the opening of *King Lear*. As I settled into my seat, my thoughts traveled back to that evening. It had been my first encounter with *King Lear*, and I hadn't liked the play at all. And then there had been that odd Mr. Grossmann backstage.

The theatre was filling up. The reviews had been good, and it was going to be nearly a full house. I smiled with satisfaction, remembering the initial response Papa had received in London. But America did love him and always remembered him, no matter what. It had been more than two weeks since President Garfield's death, and all of the unpleasantness about assassins ceased with a rapidity I found pleasantly surprising. Once again I hoped that the great accomplishments of Edwin Booth, the tragedian, would eventually diminish the notoriety of John Wilkes Booth, the assassin.

The box across from me, as prominently placed as my own, remained noticeably empty as the theatre filled. The play had almost begun when the door in the rear of the box opened and a short, well-dressed couple in late middle age entered, followed by a younger man and woman. A murmur rippled through the audience as they appeared, followed a moment later by a spontaneous burst of applause. Only then did I realize that the bearded, somewhat stubby-looking man across from me was the former president, General Grant.

General Grant bowed formally to the audience, acknowledging the applause in a studied, dignified manner. A feeling of panic began to clutch at me. Downing had told me the Grants lived in New York, and Papa's opening was a significant cultural event, so naturally they would attend. But to be seated so, directly across from me! The audience always loved to observe the occupants of the boxes, and would not fail to notice with all the recent stories about assassins still fresh. Everyone knew the Grants had almost been seated with President Lincoln in his box the night he was killed. Paralyzed, I sat in my seat and prayed the lights would dim before the audience began to notice.

As I sat there, a sudden thought of protest sprang out from the back of my mind: *I don't deserve this!* Emboldened by it, I glanced across at the Grants. They were calmly settling into their seats, the General and Mrs. Grant in the front, the younger couple behind. The young man bore a striking resemblance to the General, and I guessed he was his son, the one his family called Buck. The young woman was probably his new wife, Fannie. Their wedding last year had been reported in all the papers, including those in London. Buck, who had done well for himself on Wall Street, was viewed as a nice catch for the pretty Fannie, and tonight the young couple looked very happy and serene. I wondered enviously if they would be able to sit there so complacently if their last name had a great problem attached to it the way mine did.

Within seconds, another pointed murmur began to ripple through the audience. I listened with dread as it gathered momentum. *But I've done nothing*, I silently protested. I glanced down, and sure enough, many faces were turned up to me, some looking back and forth between the Grants' box and my own. My heart began to pound as the murmured words "Booth's daughter" slowly became distinct to my ears. *Edwin* Booth's daughter! I wanted to shout back. But I could only stare helplessly ahead of me, directly at the Grants' box.

Mrs. Grant suddenly became aware of the second stirring of the audience, and she began to look around. As she did so, her daughter-in-law leaned forward and whispered in her ear. Mrs. Grant looked across at me and smiled kindly. She appeared to think for a moment, then turned to her husband and quietly said something. General Grant nodded and slowly rose to his feet. An immediate hush came over the entire theatre. My heart pounded madly. General Grant stepped forward to the edge of the box, looked over at me, and bowed, a respectful, polite acknowledgment of the presence of the daughter of the artist of the evening.

Once again, the audience burst into applause, but this time for me, the daughter of their beloved Edwin Booth. A strange mixture of relief and pride welled up in my breast. I nodded my head to General Grant, and he returned to his seat. Beside him Mrs. Grant was still smiling across at me, and I knew that the respectful tribute had been prompted by her instant understanding of the embarrassing nature of the situation. I smiled back at her, hoping to convey some of the deep gratitude I felt. Seconds later the lights dimmed, and *Othello* began.

"But the applause was really for you," I told Papa after the performance. I would not have mentioned the incident to him, but he had already learned of it from a stagehand. So I told him when he asked, but I left out that the true reason for General Grant's bow was his wife's kind concern over my being embarrassed by people who remembered something about John Wilkes Booth. "It was simply a token of esteem," I lied.

"Frankly, I'm surprised they were here," he said. "Do you remember my friend Adam Badeau?"

"General Badeau? I've heard you speak of him, but if I've met him I can't remember."

"You may not have met him. I haven't seen much of him in recent years. Mary doesn't care for him." He paused, remembering. "Adam's been very close to the Grants. He was an important aide to Grant during the war, and afterward during his presidency. He knows them well, and he's told me they have little interest in the theatre. They were probably here for social reasons. Were they alone?"

"Their son and his wife were with them." I thought of the dowdy Mrs. Grant's kind smile. "They all looked very nice."

Papa played at Booth's Theatre until the end of October, then went to Haverly's Theatre in Brooklyn for a week. Afterward, he and the rest of the company and I departed for the Lyceum

Theatre in Philadelphia, the tour's first stop. The morning after we opened we were having breakfast alone in the dining room of our hotel when Papa abruptly said, "Mary died this morning."

"Papa," I asked gently, "you've heard from New York?"

"The news will come today."

"Then how do you know?"

"I dreamed of her."

I simply looked at him, not knowing what to say. I knew nothing of the meaning of dreams. We finished the meal in silence.

Early that afternoon a black-bordered cable arrived for Papa. He opened it, read it quickly, and passed it to me. Mama was indeed gone. She had died at five o'clock that morning.

The wake and funeral service were to be at the McVickers' house in New York. After that, the body would be taken to Chicago for burial. "I had hoped she'd have wanted to be buried in Boston, next to our child," Papa said sadly. There was no bitterness in his voice, but there was in mine when I replied, "It was her parents who decided on Chicago, I'm sure." Papa didn't know that for many weeks before her death Mama had been in no condition to make decisions.

Performances were canceled while we traveled to New York. I watched Papa closely, waiting for signs of the dreaded black mood to appear. But Papa's usual calmness and restraint did not deepen or change. In Philadelphia before we left, he accepted the condolences of members of the company with polite gravity, usually responding, "She'd been sick a very long time, and her release is now a blessing." The only dismay or anxiety he voiced on the train ride to New York was over the possibility that the McVickers would create a scene at the wake or funeral. I, too, remained perfectly calm. I had recently wondered with vague apprehension what effect Mama's death would have on me when it occurred. What I now discovered was that I had already made my peace with her that afternoon in her lace-covered bedroom.

Her body was laid out in the small foyer between two drawing rooms in the house on West Fifty-fourth Street. The mortician had done his work well, skillfully erasing the ravages of illness, and Mama looked younger and healthier in death than she had during the final decade of her life. The first thing I saw when I stepped up to the casket with Papa was my string of pearls around Mama's neck. I felt not possessiveness, but a quiet sense of victory. In seizing complete control of the funeral arrangements and choice of gravesite, the McVickers had attempted to exclude Papa and me, to erase us from Mama's life. Obviously they did not know the source of the pearls or they would not have wanted her to be buried wearing them.

Papa stood for a long while looking down at Mama's body. Finally he sighed wearily, turned away, and went back into the receiving room. I lingered a bit longer. I was about to move away when a loud voice coming from the opposite room stopped me. It was unmistakably the voice of Mrs. McVicker. "Her gown," she was telling someone, "was made from material she had me buy during the summer. The poor dear wanted it for a costume. *He* had deluded her into believing she would act with him in some play they had seen in London. Something about a cup. Such a cruel thing to do to her. So very cruel."

I frowned in disgust. The woman was still spreading her lies, even at her daughter's wake. But my frown faded, replaced by a secretive smile when I once more glanced down at my pearls.

Both drawing rooms became very crowded as many people came to pay their respects. Papa's mood grew heavier after viewing Mama's body, and although he remained calm he was mostly silent, sitting rather stiffly on a chair near the casket. Fearing that the black mood was upon him, I sat next to him, holding his hand. It was I who spoke with and thanked those who came to offer their condolences. On my other side sat Downing; his tall frame looked uncomfortable and awkward on the tiny chair. From time to time I whispered to him, encouraging him to go find a more comfortable seat or to step outside for a smoke, but he remained. When he went to view the body, he stayed there nearly as long as Papa and I, although he had never met Mama.

My thoughts had just wandered away from Downing when I looked up to see a man with red hair striding across the room toward us. Middle-aged and thick-bodied, he walked with a formal carriage that spoke of the military. His ruddy face wore a dour, serious expression, and his clothing was neat and primly detailed. As he drew closer I saw that the strangely metallic look to his red hair was due to its being streaked with gray.

I smiled politely and prepared to greet him, but as he reached us he seemed to see only Papa. "My dear friend," he said, pronouncing each word precisely.

Papa, who had not seen him approaching, looked up with a start. A second later I felt the hand of his I was holding relax and slip from my grip as he stood up solemnly and shook the man's hand. "Oh, Adam," he groaned, and I understood that the red-haired man was his friend Adam Badeau.

Papa turned to me. "This, Adam, is the child of the one who left me years ago."

General Badeau turned a pair of blue eyes toward me. "A strong resemblance, I see."

"Yes," whispered Papa. His face was now wet with tears.

With no change in his dour expression, General Badeau

looked again at me. "I knew your mother," he said. Then he managed a little smile, and I understood that smiling was something he seldom did. I smiled back pleasantly.

Papa wept frequently through the remainder of the wake, yet clearly his descent into the black mood had been arrested by the arrival of his friend. The silence and withdrawal he had begun after viewing Mama's body had stopped, and he began to speak freely of his grief with those around him. Even the eulogy, given by a friend of the McVickers and filled with innuendo, did not cause a recurrence, and directly after it Papa decided that, accompanied by General Badeau and a few other friends, he would travel to Chicago to see the body interred. I was to remain in New York with Downing's family and then rejoin Papa later in Philadelphia.

The next morning Downing and I were alone in the parlor of the Vaux apartment, consulting timetables for my train trip back to Philadelphia, when I noticed he was looking at me curiously. I asked what he was thinking.

"About you. About how steady and composed you were yesterday. You didn't grieve the way your father did. At first I thought you must have been very distant from your stepmother. Being at the wake didn't seem difficult for you at all. You could have been at an afternoon party."

I looked away. "It was difficult."

"I know. I saw your face when they closed the casket, and I knew then that you'd loved her. But even then you were so calm. Almost as if you were just watching a child being tucked into bed for the night. You didn't seem to feel any of the horror or ugliness of it."

"I did feel it," I said quietly.

He stared at me. "You felt that? And still you remained so calm?"

"I just ignore those feelings and they go away."

"But don't they frighten you?" His voice was barely a whisper.

"No."

"Why not?"

"I don't know. They just don't." I reached out and placed my hand on his. "You feel these things too deeply."

He grasped my hand, interlocking our fingers. Then, for the first time, he kissed me on the lips, and I felt as though some deep part of myself was being drawn out to him. For a moment we remained so, our lips touching, our hands interlocked; then he pulled away. "Edwina," he said, and made a slight move to return to me, but stopped. "I must work now," he whispered and rushed from the room.

When he was gone I felt very lightheaded, almost dizzy. The feeling, although odd, was not altogether unpleasant, and I suspected it was caused by my excitement over my first kiss. I once felt the same way at school after standing too long on line. That day I almost fainted, and the Sister in charge made me place my head down between my knees to stabilize my circulation. It would never do for me to faint in the Vaux family's parlor, so I sat down and bent forward. As I did so, I recalled a line from a popular song about how being in love could make a person dizzy.

A great many letters of condolence had been sent to our hotel in Philadelphia, and when I returned later in the week I immediately set about reading and acknowledging them. One letter, written on plain white stationery, was from Mr. Ignatius Grossmann. "Although I had the honor of meeting Mrs. Booth on only one occasion, backstage after the opening of *King Lear*," he wrote, "I liked her very much. I sincerely enjoyed the time I spent

with her." He added, "On that same occasion I also had the pleasure of meeting Miss Booth. I understand she is now engaged, and
I respectfully offer my congratulations." Because I barely knew
him, I did not write a personal note on the back of the printed
card I sent, thanking him for his letter of sympathy.

Papa returned from Chicago in reasonably good spirits, anxious to work and get on with the American tour. "And next year,
on to Germany and Austria," he told me with a smile, and I was
pleased he was thinking of the future with optimism. Outside
of briefly describing Mama's Chicago gravesite to me when he
first returned, his thoughts didn't seem to linger on her death,
and he seldom spoke of it. I could only hope the knowledge that
Mama's torment was finally ended had ultimately been as great
a comfort to him as it was to me.

At the end of the Philadelphia engagement we boarded the
special railroad car that Mr. Abbey had arranged for the tour.
There was a large Pullman for the company, while Papa and I
traveled in a connecting car of our own. Mr. Abbey insisted that
Papa be as comfortable as possible for the six months he would
be living in the car, and it had been well furnished, including
armchairs and a piano. It had dining space for at least eight
people, and small but sufficient quarters for three servants.

In mid-November the trial of Charles Guiteau for the assassination of President Garfield began. All the newspapers reported on
it. Fortunately for the Booth family, Charles Guiteau, who was
clearly insane, behaved so wildly that the press found no need to
dig up supporting material, and the name of John Wilkes Booth
was, for the most part, left alone.

After reading all the stories about Guiteau's behavior I realized it had been a very merciful thing that my uncle had died

before being brought to trial. During the past summer when all the old stories about John Wilkes Booth were brought up, I read that most people considered him to have been mad. With horror, I wondered how Papa would have survived a similar courtroom display on the part of his brother.

In early February we reached New Orleans, the halfway and turning point of the tour. The past months had seen us travel west from Philadelphia through Pennsylvania into Ohio, then south through Kentucky, Tennessee, Mississippi, and Louisiana. After the two-night stopover in New Orleans we traveled north again, stopping at cities not included on the route during the trip south.

After New Orleans, I began to find the tour insufferably boring. There were endless stops in places that held no interest for me. The luxurious train car began to feel like a prison, a gilded cage from which I longed to escape. I was frequently irritable. Once, when I passed before a mirror, I was appalled to see how pinched and angular my face appeared. I began to count the days until the tour's conclusion in April.

Papa, on the other hand, was flourishing under the same conditions I found so trying. His health was excellent, his spirits high, his energy soaring. Nearly every night he asked different members of the company to join us for dinner in the hotel car, and he planned incessant small excursions, picnics, and sightseeing trips in any town where there was a stopover. He frequently asked me to play the piano or read aloud to him.

I noted the difference between us. His buoyancy was generated through his work. His personal elevation of mood corresponded to periods of intense creativity. A true artist, Papa was always happiest when performing. At those times he was capable of absorbing the energy of an admiring audience and using it for sustenance and rejuvenation. In light of this understanding I finally felt comfortable broaching the subject of his upcoming tour of Germany.

"Papa, do you think you could manage to go to Germany without me?"

He looked up from the book he was reading. "You don't wish to come?"

"It's not that I don't wish to. But with my wedding coming up I have so many preparations to make."

"I hadn't thought of that." He massaged the bridge of his nose. "Mary would have, though. She always knew all about those things. She was such a help raising you."

"I know, Papa." I felt a pang of sadness. Mama would have loved planning the wedding, and would have done so to perfection. "There's a lot to do, actually. I have no linens, nothing." Suddenly I was afraid that I would not be able to handle everything alone. I wished desperately that Mama were still alive, even as she had been during the final difficult years of her life.

"Where would you stay?"

"At Long Branch, with Grandma." Now that President Garfield was gone, Long Branch had lost its unpleasantness for me. "And Downing can visit me there."

He glanced out the window at the passing cotton fields of Tennessee. "I had thought to ask him to come along to Germany with us. But now I see you are right—there is much to prepare. Perhaps it would be better for you to remain in Long Branch. Grandma and Aunt Rosalie can help you."

This thought was ludicrous indeed. Did he not understand

how aged and tired his mother was, how withdrawn his sister? But I was delighted he agreed so easily to let me remain in America. Now I would have ample time for the wedding preparations. There was always Downing's mother for help, and Julia. Feeling more in control, I sat down to write Downing the good news that the issue was settled. I felt better and more at ease than I had for the past several days.

Downing's letters came less frequently than they had during our first long separation, and the ones that did come provided less relief from the monotony of the tour. Yet I did not mind. Somehow, being on the same continent, not separated by a vast ocean, made me feel much closer to him than I had in London. And I felt a great security in being engaged. Whenever the hardships and discomforts of the tour became particularly intolerable, I found solace in the thoughts of my upcoming marriage. Just as in London a year before, however, I was at times troubled by a curious inability to remember what Downing looked like.

I could never have accompanied you to Germany, Downing wrote to me. *Your father was generous to offer to take me, but I am much too busy here to take a prolonged trip. Naturally, though, I am happy you will be staying in Long Branch.*

Ever so slowly the tour worked its way north to its conclusion. At the beginning of April, while we were in Chicago, our last major stop, we read in the newspapers of the proposed sale of Booth's Theatre. Someone, it seemed, wanted to destroy the theatre by turning it into a store.

My first reaction was to try to conceal the reports from Papa, but the effort was futile, as the rest of the company was discussing it. And of course he would have to know sooner or later. "It's terrible!" I said when I finally mentioned it to him. I did conceal reports that were critical of him. Most stories reported that the theatre had never been a moneymaker, pointing out that even Papa had gone bankrupt there.

By April we were in New York, where Papa performed at Booth's Theatre for the last time. Immediately after the close of the engagement we took a day trip to Long Branch to visit our relatives and to make final plans for my stay.

I was grateful for the opportunity to get Papa away from New York City. He was looking forward to his European tour, but lately there had been a slight tension about him, a small discordant note of unease in his demeanor. It was not definable, nor was it visible to others; Downing said he saw nothing. But I was certain of it. He had performed at Booth's Theatre for the last time. I hated to think what his mood would be if he were not concluding one highly successful tour and setting out on another. The sooner he was away from Booth's Theatre and New York City, the better, and until then the short trip to Long Branch was a welcome diversion.

Although Grandma Booth's exact age was unknown to her children and grandchildren, we all assumed that by 1882 she was close to eighty. If one were judging solely by her looks one would possibly guess that she was even older. She had once possessed great beauty and vitality, people said, but now she seemed withered and tired. Her hair was white, her shoulders stooped, her face lined with wrinkles. She walked slowly and with difficulty, using a cane. Oddly, I had trouble remembering a time when she looked different. My relatives said Grandma had barely aged at all until President Lincoln's assassination but had then become an old woman overnight.

She spent a good part of each day sitting and looking out the front parlor window onto Ocean Avenue, and that was where we found her when we arrived. As we came up the front path we saw her small, round face staring out at us. When she saw us she raised her hand in a little wave of greeting, but the gesture seemed weak and halfhearted. Inside, she greeted us more exuberantly, kissing Papa and stroking his hair, and pinching my cheek and saying, "I keep forgetting what a big girl Edwina's gotten to be."

Papa laughed. "This big girl is getting married soon, Mother."

Aunt Rosalie, silent as usual, came in and seemed genuinely glad to see us, especially me. "I'll be staying here the whole time Papa's in Europe," I whispered to her. She smiled.

I opened the bundle of gifts I had bought for them during our trip through the South—a brightly colored cotton shawl from Mississippi for Grandmother, and for Aunt Rosalie, a small painting of a traditional plantation house. "And where's Uncle Joe?" I asked, taking out the box of fine Virginia tobacco I planned to give him.

"He'll be home for dinner," said Grandma. "He said he would definitely be here." She glanced nervously at Aunt Rosalie. I couldn't imagine why.

Just before dinner Uncle Joe arrived. Right away I noticed a significant change in him. I had memories of playing and laughing with him when I was a child, but in recent years I had known only a moody, withdrawn, sullen man, drifting into a middle age full of eccentricity. Physically, he resembled his brothers for the most part, although his dark features were more elongated than theirs, his frame slighter. But beyond the physical, all similarities ended. Uncle Joe, the youngest in the family, was openly regarded by his siblings as the black sheep. He had no interest whatsoever in the theatre; the short time he spent as treasurer of Booth's Theatre had been disastrous. A little more successful was a series of real estate investments he made in Long Branch. From time to time he spoke of becoming a doctor, and for a while he even studied to become one, but by age forty-two he was still undecided. In many things he displayed this pronounced indecisiveness, and Papa would at times tease him about it, which only served to deepen his ever-present irritability.

The absence of this irritability was what I first noticed when he came in. He greeted us pleasantly, even calling Papa by his childhood name, Ned. Then, although I expected him to accept his gift of the tobacco without comment, he instead became full of thanks, even whistling in admiration at its quality. Surprised, I glanced at Papa's face to see if these changes in Uncle Joe were as evident to him as they were to me. I saw that they were. I saw something else, too, in Papa's expression, something that confused and troubled me, but it vanished when I looked more closely. I must have misinterpreted it. Papa could not possibly have been viewing his brother with envy.

"New suit, Joe?" Papa asked him.

"Sure is. Had a few of them made last week."

I looked at the suit, stylishly cut and of the finest material. Uncle Joe had always been known for his outdated, baggy suits, which he claimed were comfortable. "You look very nice, Uncle Joe," I said.

"Yes, he does," Papa agreed. "A whole new man." Was there a hint of mockery in his voice? No, surely his behavior was simply that of an older brother.

"I feel a whole new man," said Uncle Joe.

"To what do we owe this transformation?" asked Papa.

Uncle Joe smiled secretively. "Life."

"Yes, life's full of surprises," said Papa, and his tone clearly indicated he meant that not all of them were pleasant.

The dining room, long and narrow, was cramped and crowded when we sat down to dinner. I had never felt it so before. All through the meal I had a vaguely ominous impression that something was gathering momentum around me, storm clouds creeping in over the horizon. The others seemed to feel it too, and although I chattered, the conversation was stilted and awkward. From time to time Uncle Joe would make some silly, playful remark, and each time he did, Papa would look at him with silent suspicion.

When the maid had cleared away the dinner plates and we had started on dessert, Uncle Joe said, "I'm marrying Margaret next month, Ned."

I stared at him in surprise. Was this what accounted for the change in him, that he was getting married? He was behaving exactly the way the characters in romantic novels did when they fell in love. A few years ago I stopped reading such novels, having decided they were silly and unrealistic. But my uncle did not seem silly to me at all, only buoyant and happy. "That's wonderful, Uncle Joe," I said, with much sincerity. I wondered who this Margaret was, whom Papa already seemed to know of.

"Congratulations," Papa said blandly. He looked at Grandma. "Now that Joe's getting married, Mother, of course you and Rosalie will come live with me."

"This is our home, Edwin," she answered gently. "Rosalie and I will stay here with Joe and his new wife. We're comfortable here."

"I'll buy a house."

"No, Edwin. Rosalie and I stay here."

The storm had burst. The note of tension in Papa magnified

tenfold, and he grew rigid. Horrified, I sat fearing that at any moment an eruption of seething violence would destroy us all. Then it seemed to peak, and stabilize. Papa sat very still for a few moments, his eyes on the table. With perfect calm he said, "Well, Edwina, I'm sorry there'll be no room for you here when I go to Europe."

I was shocked. "Papa" was the sole word I uttered.

Grandma saw my stricken look. "Of course there's still room for her."

"No," Papa interrupted. "I've decided she's coming to Europe with me."

"There's room," whispered Aunt Rosalie. Everyone looked at her.

Uncle Joe stood up. "You won't let her stay here because of Margaret."

Papa said nothing. To me, Uncle Joe said, "Your father doesn't like her. I'm sorry. You know you're welcome here anytime." He strode out of the room.

At the end of the table Grandma bowed her head.

That night the train ride back to New York seemed to take forever. Papa sat beside me in stony silence on the uncomfortable seat in the coach car. The train was half-empty at this late hour, so when I finally ventured to speak to him, I did so with a fair amount of privacy.

"Papa, you really won't allow me to stay there?"

"No. It's impossible now."

"Grandma and Aunt Rosalie will still be there."

"Yes. That is unfortunate. When we return from Europe they'll come live with us. I'm going to buy a house before we go, so it will be all ready when we come back."

"But, Papa, Grandma said she wanted to stay there."

"Soon, Edwina, very soon, she will come to feel differently."

It was hopeless; he would never agree. One possible solution remained, and I decided to present it at once. "Can I stay with Downing's family?"

He shook his head. "I've decided it's best for you to come with me."

His tone indicated that his decision was final. Tears came to my eyes. Defeated, I rested my head on the back of the seat, staring at my reflection in the darkened window next to me. More than anything else, I dreaded telling Downing this news. I closed my eyes in an effort to hold back the tears. The train rocked rhythmically as it sped along through the night. For a moment it seemed as though I was still in the cage-like hotel car in which I had spent so many months.

"I don't want you to go." Downing sat stiffly on the edge of the sofa in the parlor of our suite at the Brunswick.

"I have to."

"You can stay with us."

"I've already asked that. He said no."

He bit his lower lip. "This is intolerable."

"Don't say that," I implored. "It would have been difficult for him to have gone alone under any circumstances. And now he's upset, hurt, and angry." I shivered a little, remembering how he had been. "I'd never seen him so upset before. It was frightening. I thought he would become ill."

"Simply because his brother is marrying someone he doesn't care for?"

I became defensive. "That's unfair, Downing. All our relatives have always depended on my father, and it's only right he should have some say in how they conduct themselves. You don't know how silly-headed Uncle Joe can be. I'm sure there's a good reason for Papa to disapprove of this woman he's marrying." Even as I said this the words sounded hollow. I could not forget how happy my uncle had looked.

"Suppose your father disapproved of me?" Downing asked softly.

My answer was quick. "He doesn't." I strained to take a deep breath. I did not feel well today, having awakened with a headache I couldn't shake. A heavy feeling had settled in my chest and was shifting into my side.

Downing leaned forward, his elbows on his knees, his head in his hands. The sight of his disappointment was almost more than I could stand.

I sat next to him and took his hand. "Downing, Downing, please be reasonable. It's not such a terrible thing, to delay a few months longer. We're young; we have our lives ahead of us. If we're patient now and make changes gently, no one will get hurt." I patted his hand. "And we must be careful not to cause a disturbance that would interfere with my father's acting. This is a very important tour, you know. England first, then Germany and Austria."

He looked up at me, and for the first time I saw a touch of coldness in his eyes. "You sound as though you want to go."

He had gone too far. Angry, I stood up. "Want to go! Are you mad? Obviously you don't know what it's like! How do you think it feels, Downing Vaux, to be dragged around from city to city, living on trains and in hotel rooms? There's never a moment's rest, never a moment to sit down and put your feet up and relax! And always having to smile for the *public*, and sit through boring teas and luncheons while silly women flutter around you saying, 'Oh, Miss Booth, this,' and 'Oh, Miss Booth, that'!" I stopped abruptly, unable to breathe, and sat back down. My head thudded dully, and the heavy feeling in my side was sharper.

"I'm sorry," said Downing. He took out his handkerchief and gave it to me so I could wipe my forehead. "Of course you don't want to go," he said distantly. "After we're married, you'll never have to travel anywhere. We'll settle down. And then I'll be able to paint masterpieces."

"Can't you come with us?" I whispered.

"No." He went rigid. "I explained that to you. I have things I can't just ignore. Things that in their own way are just as important as acting." Determination crossed his face. "I'm going to speak with your father about allowing you to stay with us."

Panic gripped me. If he confronted Papa in his present mood, the result could be disastrous. "No, Downing, not now."

"He's a reasonable man. And he's going to be my father-in-law. Don't worry, I'll be very polite."

I felt too weak to argue. "At least wait a few days," I murmured.

"All right. A few days."

He stood up and walked to the table by the window. On it were spread out the architectural plans for a house in Newport that his father was going to have built.

"Has your father studied these plans yet?" Downing asked.

"No, not yet. But I think he will want to buy the house. Once he decides something, he usually does it." I touched my forehead, which was starting to feel warm.

That afternoon I developed a fever. I went right to bed and Betty brought me ice packs for my head, but the fever grew worse, and by evening it was quite high. My head ached so badly I was sure it would explode, and every time I inhaled I was stabbed by pain in my side. Breathing became more and more difficult, and soon it felt as though my lungs were closing.

Nearly frantic, Papa called in two doctors to examine me. Their diagnosis was pleuropneumonia. "Serious, but we've caught it early enough," one of them reported. "With proper treatment, she'll be back up, good as new, in no time at all. A little more than two weeks and she'll be well."

Papa refused to be reassured by this diagnosis, and remained in a state of high agitation for several days. He stayed in the bedroom with me for hours on end, along with Betty and the full-time nurses, and at night he slept on the sofa in the parlor of the suite so as to be close at hand. He was utterly distraught, his thoughts completely fixed on my condition. He seemed to expect the worst. Over and over he said, "I can't bear the thought of losing her. I just can't bear it."

Fortunately I possessed a very strong constitution, and my recovery was rapid after the fever broke. Within a few days I felt much better, and as the doctor had promised, after two weeks I was back on my feet. At Papa's insistence the doctor still visited me daily, and every day I ingested countless vitamin pills and tonics.

After I had been out of bed for several days, Downing approached Papa about allowing me to stay in America while he went to Europe. "I'm going to appeal to his concern for your health," he told me. "There's no question you're over the illness, but I suspect he's not so sure of it." Although I felt a little guilty about this devious approach, I did not object.

Later, Downing told me about the conversation. "You fear a relapse?" Papa asked when Downing mentioned my health.

"It's possible," Downing replied.

"I understand," Papa said. "I fear one too. Which is why she must come with me. Suppose she were taken ill again, and I were across the ocean, and unable to come to her?" His voice had become a whisper. "Suppose she were to die before I could get there?"

"That is unlikely, sir."

"No. Those, young man, were exactly the conditions under which Edwina's mother died years ago. I couldn't get there in time."

Downing didn't reply; what could anyone have said to that?

Then Papa said, "I've already hired a private doctor to come with us on the tour. Edwina will be well attended." He added, "You do realize she'd like nothing better than for you to come with us."

But Downing replied that he could not.

As I listened to the account of this conversation I grew concerned about Papa. I hadn't realized my illness reminded him of another of the great sorrows of his life. "Well, that settles it now," I said when Downing finished. "If I don't go, he'll be mad with worry the whole time. He'll never be able to act in that condition. It will be disastrous; he might as well cancel the whole trip if I don't go with him." I looked at Downing with resignation. "The last time he had this opportunity, he lost it because my stepmother was ill. I can't be the reason for him to lose it again. Surely you can understand that."

After a moment he said, "Yes, I do understand." His voice had no expression. "You could never hurt your father by going against his wishes."

"I couldn't." Strangely, I felt as though I were admitting to some severe defect of character.

"Hurting him would be more than you could stand." He said this not as an accusation but rather as a simple statement of fact.

"You know I don't want to go."

He smiled sadly. In an odd, soothing tone, he said, "Poor Edwina. Never wants to hurt anyone, or disappoint anyone. Always so willing to comply." He cleared his throat. "Your father is going to ask my sister to go with you."

"Julia! Oh, that would be wonderful, the next best thing to having you come! It will be like having a little piece of you with me. Do you think she'll say yes?"

"I can't see why not. There's never been anything to keep her from doing what she pleases." Sullenly, he added, "No one's ever expected of her what they expect of me."

Delighted with the invitation, Julia accepted, and at once I began to view the trip in a much more favorable light. After all, this time we would not be confined in a cage-like rail car, and we would be traveling to some of the most sophisticated cities in Europe, not primitive Southern towns. Having Julia along would be truly the next best thing to having Downing there. Although Julia and her brother were almost exact opposites in temperament, I felt that being for an extended period of time with a member of the family I was marrying into would be an excellent way of preparing for the marriage. I was to be separated from Downing for almost a year, but that time would not be an utter waste.

Downing seemed to have resigned himself to our separation as well. After his conversation with Papa, he never again raised the subject. If he was more silent than usual in the days before Papa and I left, I reasoned it was only natural. I, too, was sad at the thought of our being apart. But there were so many details to attend to before leaving, I simply didn't have time to dwell on my feelings.

Before we departed, Papa took a short trip to Newport to examine the site for the house Calvert Vaux had designed. Upon his return, he bought it, and construction began. "It will be ready when we return, and Grandma and Aunt Rosalie can move right in," he told me. I made no comment. Grandma had written me that Uncle Joe had gone ahead with his marriage. She wrote that she found his new wife "charming and gracious." Clearly, Grandma had no intention of moving out because of her.

On June 14, 1882, Papa, Julia, Betty, Dr. St. Clair Smith, and I settled into our rooms on the liner *Gallia*. Downing helped us board, then went to wait with the crowd on the pier. Julia and I went up on deck and waved to him as we sailed, remaining there until we could no longer make out his face in the crowd.

FOUR   1882

Christmas Day dawned dreary and gray over London, the air damp and cold. Little flurries of snow began in midafternoon, and by evening thick flakes fell heavily. I stood by a window in the parlor of our suite at the Moxley Hotel, watching as the descending mass of white shifted and billowed in the wind. In the parlor behind me, the Yule log crackled in the fireplace. The room was festive and comfortably warm, and with a shudder I turned back to it gladly, away from the window. The falling snow suddenly seemed a great web—or a shroud—settling over the city.

At the table, Papa and Julia were playing dominoes for what seemed to me to be the thousandth time since the trip began. Papa had taken to Julia's vivacious manner and cheerful spirits. Our ship had not been one day out to sea before it became apparent that they would get along famously. Although I'd never noticed it before, Julia in many ways resembled the way Mama was during the first years of her marriage to Papa. She was small, pert, darkly pretty, and energetic. This afternoon she and Papa had been at their game since right after Christmas dinner, and it showed no signs of ending soon.

Behind them, in an armchair by the fireplace, sat Downing, his lap covered by a woolen shawl. Two months ago I would have been overjoyed at the prospect of having him with us for

Christmas. Now as I looked at him I would a thousand times prefer that he were back in America, well and happy, rather than sitting here with me in this reduced, apathetic condition.

During the first months of Papa's tour in England, Downing's letters to me were scarce, less frequent even than during the year when Papa and I toured the South, and then in November the letters ceased entirely. Two weeks later a letter came from Calvert Vaux, explaining that Downing had been seriously injured in an accident. Apparently he neglected to extinguish the gas jets he was not using in his room one evening, and several hours later he was found unconscious, overcome by fumes. He had almost died, and only with great difficulty had he been revived. Since then his physical health had stabilized, but his mind had been profoundly affected. Although he suffered no distortions of reality, he was in a perpetual state of sadness. Mentally, he was lethargic and depressed. Nothing could rouse or cheer him. If art was so much as mentioned, he would turn away and weep.

I became almost mad with fear when I learned of the accident, crying out that it was all my fault for not staying in America. Eventually Papa and Julia were able to calm me, and Papa pointed out that it would have occurred no matter where I was. The important thing was that Downing had survived. He was being treated by competent physicians and would no doubt get well. Papa and Julia both believed this, and so I decided they must be right. But I was unable to rid myself entirely of the feeling that if I had remained in America, the accident would not have occurred. Shortly after the accident it was decided that Downing would join us in Europe. His being with me, everyone reasoned, would surely have a healing effect upon him and elevate his spirits.

He arrived just before Christmas. I almost cried at the apathetic greeting I received from him. "Give him a few days," Papa whispered to me. So I had, but now a few days had passed with no improvement. Papa and Julia were both confident he would soon be well, but I did not share their optimism. Only I seemed to recognize how deeply his illness was entrenched. Consequently, I alone seemed to have shouldered the burden of responsibility for his recovery.

I glanced over at Papa and Julia, happily playing a silly game while just across the room Downing sat in silence. A quick surge of resentment flashed through me at their apparent indifference to his suffering. But then, it was only natural that I would be more sensitive to his condition than anyone else. It was I who was to be his spouse. I went over to him and tucked the blanket more tightly around his legs. "Are you warm enough?" I asked gently. He nodded in reply.

"Edwina, why don't you and Downing play the next game with us?" called Julia. Papa looked up and smiled.

"Would you like to play dominoes?" I asked Downing.

"No," he said in a feeble voice.

"Perhaps later," I told Julia.

I pulled another armchair over next to Downing's and sat down. The high, upholstered backs of the chairs formed a sort of screen between us and Papa and Julia.

I reached over and patted his knee. "I'm so glad you're here," I whispered.

I did not expect a reply to this statement; I thought that at most he might nod a little. Therefore, I was utterly startled when after a moment he whispered hoarsely, "He won."

"Won? Who won?" I whispered back.

"Your father."

I could hear the urgency in his barely audible voice. "What do you mean?"

Again, several moments passed while he stared into the fire. I waited, my heart pounding, dreading that he would now lapse back into apathy. I did not understand his last remark, and it seemed crucial that I do so.

Finally he whispered, "He wanted me to come. I'm here." He looked at me, and for the first time since his arrival I saw clarity in his eyes. "He always gets his way," he continued.

I was appalled. "No, Downing!"

He closed his eyes. "I can't."

"Can't what?"

"Have another."

"Another what?"

"Famous, accomplished father."

"Why?"

"It's too much. It would crush me." It appeared to require some intense effort, some heroic muster of strength, for him to utter these words even as a feeble whisper. Having done so, he at once sank back into lethargy.

I grasped his hand. "No, no, no," I whispered. And then, in an instant, I understood. I suddenly knew what I had never known before, the intense pressure Downing always felt from his father's accomplishments. Sons were expected to follow in their fathers' footsteps, and possibly surpass them. They were expected to be their fathers' children. Calvert Vaux was regarded as an immensely talented man, even a genius, by some. How could one possibly follow in the footsteps of a genius?

My thoughts raced back over so many incidents, so many places where I should have seen the effects of this tormenting pressure in Downing. What a fool I had been! And now that I saw it, was it too late? Desperately I reviewed the situation. He was away from his father, which was good. But it was absolutely urgent that I make him see that my father was different, that he would never, as Downing feared, crush him. Before I could even whisper a word to this effect, into my mind came the thought of Papa's own son, Edgar, Mama's child who had died at birth from a crushed skull. *Crushed. Crushed.* Now, over and over that word began to echo in my mind.

"Oh, my, just look at that snow coming down," said Julia, behind us.

"Perhaps it's a blizzard," Papa said, unconcerned.

Crushed.

There was never any question that Papa would open his German tour with *Hamlet*. Whereas Shakespeare was regarded with, at best, a mild respect by the French, who vastly preferred the more formal works of their own Racine, Corneille, and Molière, the Germans adored the works of the English playwright. They were held in as high esteem in Germany as they were in England, regarded as the equal of anything written by Goethe or Schiller. In Germany, Shakespeare's plays were frequently performed in the theatres, taught in all the classrooms, studied, and read for pleasure. And of all the plays, *Hamlet*, the story of the melancholy Prince of Denmark, was the most cherished.

The Residenz Theatre in Berlin, small and intimate, had been chosen for the opening. Papa, who spoke no German, would perform in English, while the rest of the company would speak in German. Even with so difficult a manner of performing, no more than two weeks could be allotted for rehearsals. All too soon, on the night of January 11, 1883, the curtain rose.

I was seated with Downing and Julia in one of the Residenz's few small boxes as the theatre slowly filled with polite, orderly Berlin citizens for the opening. I was utterly exhausted. With Downing's arrival the tour had gone from being a time of relaxation to one of constant stress and anxiety, in many ways worse than the previous year's tour of the South. Downing required my constant attention. Also, since our arrival in Germany, I bore the additional burden of being the only one of our party who spoke and understood the language to any degree. A hundred times a day I was called upon to translate. I did all the speaking to clerks in stores, all the ordering from menus in restaurants. There were times I wanted to scream.

Downing's recovery now seemed more likely than it had when he first arrived. With sustained effort on my part, he would soon be fully well, and we could proceed with our life together as we intended. There would, of course, have to be some changes. Removing Downing from his father's sphere would take effort, but I didn't doubt that it could be done. Papa would help us. I envisioned settling into a little apartment, in a city where few people had ever heard of Calvert Vaux or Central Park. Downing would no longer stand in his father's shadow, and he would be free of the dreary mundane concerns of handling his business for him. What he needed now was a place where his own artistic spirit would be free to develop, where he could start to paint.

I turned and smiled at him, seated behind me in the box. In a few days I would speak to him about my plans. I hadn't yet, because I had been warned of his adverse reaction to the subject of art, but I was confident that in a day or two I could safely bring it up.

The house lights dimmed and the curtain rose on the actors in the introductory scene, the battlements of Elsinore. The familiar lines sounded odd spoken in a foreign language. I had always admired the beauty of Shakespeare's words, the poetry of his language. Most of this was lost in translation. But what remained, the thoughts, seemed to have doubled in meaning. The top, pretty layer had been peeled away, exposing the hard truths of meaning beneath. In translation the play seemed harsher, but also more direct and clear.

The applause when Papa first came onto the stage was restrained. Nonetheless, I felt my usual pride, mixed tonight with gratification. At long last, Papa was performing on a German stage! It was the fulfillment of a dream too long deferred.

The air in the theatre was charged with expectancy as Papa stood silently, awaiting his cue to speak. Then, with brooding intensity, came his first line, "A little more than kin, and less than kind." The effect of the English words was startling, the meaning plunging directly into the souls of the listeners. They sat riveted. Surrounded by the harsher, more clipped-sounding German, the English sounded lighter and more delicate, the poetry ringing through. The effect was that this Hamlet seemed very different from those around him, a superior, godlike creature endeavoring to interact with mere mortals.

The German audience upheld a dignified reserve throughout the performance. Applause at the scene changes and intermissions was firm but restrained. Yet their rapt attention whenever Papa was on stage showed how deeply impressed they were. The connection between star and audience, the flow of energy back and forth between them, was palpable, nearly electric. I marveled at the great restraint as time and again this force was sublimated into polite applause.

Finally, Hamlet drew his last breath, and the curtain came down. One protracted moment of utter silence passed while the audience sat in darkness. Then, somewhere in the house, a woman sobbed. As if on cue, the entire audience burst into thunderous applause.

The curtain rose on the company, with Papa in the center. He was pushed forward; the applause intensified. All in the audience rose to their feet. "Bravo! Bravo!" shouted an old man near me, and the cry was taken up throughout the theatre. Some women ran up the aisles with bouquets of flowers and thrust them onto the stage. Individual flowers rained down from the balconies. "Booth! Booth!" screamed a woman in a box as she pounded her fists on the railing. Looking down, I saw that the entire orchestra section was full of waving handkerchiefs. My heart began to pound with excitement. All around, the audience was in a virtual frenzy of adoration for Papa. Cries of "Booth! Booth!" and "Herr Meister! Meister!" rang out.

The curtain fell, but the calls continued, the frenzy unabated. Papa reappeared. I felt a little fear. It was too strong, too much energy, all directed at Papa. I feared for his safety should it get out of control. But when he stepped out onstage I saw I had nothing to fear. Far from being overwhelmed, he looked confident and exhilarated, the way he always did after a fine performance. The huge waves of adoration being directed at him did not frighten him at all. On the contrary, they seemed to nourish him. He was in total, complete control.

Papa returned to the stage twenty-four times while the ovation continued. Finally it waned somewhat, and the house lights came up. Still energized and excited, the audience leaped up and began to rush out of the theatre. Their previous polite and restrained behavior dissolved as they pushed and shoved their way to the exits.

I stood and turned, and saw then the ashen color of

Downing's face. I knew at once that the wild ovation had disturbed him deeply, bringing to the surface the very things that were troubling him. Silently, I cursed myself for not anticipating this, for not keeping him away from opening night. It was urgent that we get him back to the hotel in as quiet a manner as possible. "I think we should wait until the theatre clears out a little before we go," I told Julia.

"Yes," she agreed. "Let's wait."

Downing sat staring mutely ahead. Very calmly I said, "Let's all go right back to the hotel and have a nice cup of chocolate." I called an usher and sent a message to Papa that we would not be coming backstage.

The theatre was almost empty by the time we went downstairs to the lobby. I asked the doorman to get us a carriage. A few minutes later he returned, saying that he had found one but that the size of the crowd gathered near the stage door at the end of the street made it impossible for the carriage to pass by.

"Is there another exit?" I asked him. "I'm Mr. Booth's daughter. My friends and I wish to avoid the crowd."

"No, there is only the stage door, with the huge crowd around it."

Leaving Downing with Julia, I went back outside to look. Indeed, a huge crowd, a mob, had gathered by the door from which Papa would shortly emerge. But there was a clear space behind it through which we could quietly pass to the carriage. I went back in and asked the doorman to run and hold the carriage for us.

I linked my arm through Downing's. "The carriage is just a short way down the street," I said with forced lightness. "A little walk in the fresh air will do us good." The three of us went outside and began to make our way to the carriage, steering clear of the crowd by the stage door. Fortunately, the mob faced away from us, diligently watching the door, and I was confident we could slip past without being drawn into it.

We were just beginning to pass it when I heard the first word in German. Even before my mind could translate "daughter," the entire crowd had wheeled around to look at us. Downing stopped. "Oh, no," murmured Julia. Instinctively, as though to ward off a blow, I raised my hand in front of me. And then the crowd surged toward us.

"Get away!" I shrieked, unable to control myself as the crowd engulfed us. "I can't breathe!" I heard Julia cry as her face disappeared behind a sea of extended hands. A blond woman with a large face repeatedly kissed my cheek. Bouquets of flowers were thrust at us from all directions. Glancing up, I saw Downing's face, a mask, bland and rigid.

Suddenly I was furious. "Get out of the way!" I shouted. But it was no use; all around us were the frenzied admirers of Edwin Booth. From somewhere a hand sprang out and pinched my cheek. "Booth! Booth!" a voice cooed grotesquely in my ear.

Then, by purest chance, I happened to catch a glimpse of the carriage waiting beyond the sea of heads in front of us. The sight of it strengthened me, and holding tightly to Downing, I gave a great push forward. A small space cleared. I forged through, pulling Downing and Julia behind me. Ruthlessly I shoved aside a young woman who stepped in my way. A second later I was at the carriage. Frightened by the mob, the horse tried to bolt, but the driver steadied it. The crowd swarmed around us as I pulled open the door and shoved Downing and Julia inside. I don't understand, I thought distractedly. I'm not even an actress.

I climbed in and tried to close the door. The crowd pressing against it held it open. "Just drive!" I shouted in German at the driver. As I sat down a huge bouquet came flying through the door and hit me squarely in the face. Vehemently I kicked it back out as the carriage lurched away.

A few people ran along beside for a short distance, but for the most part the mob's attention shifted back to the stage door. Soon the mob was behind us, and I reached out and pulled the carriage door shut. I gave the driver the address of the hotel, then sank back wearily on the seat. A profound exhaustion settled over me. Numbly, I stared across at Downing and Julia. I would have liked nothing better than to curl up on the seat and go to sleep.

"The boy who got us the carriage must have told them who you are," said Julia. "I certainly hope they don't do the same thing to your father."

"Oh, he likes it," I murmured, thoughtlessly. I glanced at Downing; his face looked blank. I knew I should speak to him, make some attempt to draw him out before he retreated even further within himself. But I simply could not. I felt drained and numb, incapable of uttering even a single word of support.

The ride to the hotel was mercifully quick. In the lobby, I once again sensed the urgency of Downing's need. But tonight I could not respond. I craved sleep as though some powerful narcotic had been administered to me. I was so tired that I did not know if I would be able to get upstairs to my room.

"Shall we have our chocolate now?" asked Julia.

"I'm sorry, I can't," I said. My voice sounded far away. "I have to go to sleep now. I'm very tired. I'm sorry, I have to. Good night, Julia. Good night, Downing." Clutching the banister, I staggered up the stairs to my room.

When I awoke the next morning, I had no recollection of actually getting undressed and into bed. Betty had been there, of course, as always ready to help me. Thank goodness for Betty! Over the past few weeks she alone seemed to remember that not too long ago I had been very ill. She voiced fears of a recurrence owing to exhaustion. But Dr. Smith had long since been dispensed with, and the others seemed simply to have forgotten. Fortunately, my health had been holding up satisfactorily, despite the stress.

The night's rest had done me good. I sat up and stretched, feeling refreshed and relaxed. I smiled as I remembered the stunning success of the previous evening. Papa had finally achieved the European triumph that he had always hoped for. Then I remembered Downing, and the condition I left him in the night before. Anxiety gripped me, and a sickening sense of foreboding. I slid out of bed.

Betty came in. "You slept late this morning, missy. That's good—you needed it."

"What time is it?"

"Ten o'clock."

"Are the others up yet?"

"Miss Julia and your papa are having breakfast in the dining room."

"Where's Mr. Vaux?"

"He's not awake yet."

My anxiety sharpened into outright fear. "Go wake him right now. Tell him I want to have breakfast with him."

She hurried out. Without washing, I began to pull on items of clothing. I was nearly dressed by the time she returned.

"No answer, missy. Maybe he got up early and went out." She noticed I was dressed. "Missy, you can't wear those clothes."

"I must hurry. Mr. Vaux may be ill. Quick, help me put up my hair."

Papa and Julia were eating muffins and jam when I arrived downstairs. A stack of German newspapers were on the table between them. "Ah, here's our translator now," said Papa when he saw me.

"Have either of you seen Downing?" I asked abruptly.

"He's still sleeping," said Julia. She spread some jam on a muffin.

"No, he's not." I stopped speaking as a small group of middle-aged German women passed by, smiling at Papa. He smiled and nodded at them, and they continued on. I lowered my voice. "I sent Betty to wake him, but he didn't answer. You know he wouldn't have gone out!"

Julia put down her spoon. "I do hope he's not ill again," she said vaguely.

I stared at her. "Again? Did you think he had recovered? You saw how ill he was last night!" To Papa I said, "The crowd disturbed him."

Papa frowned. "Let me think," he said.

Anxiety clawed at me. "Hurry, Papa! Let's get the hotel manager to open the door, break it down if necessary!"

"No," he said sharply. "Nothing that would attract attention. It will end up in all the papers, just as with Mary in London." He stood up. "Maybe Betty didn't knock loudly enough. Let me try."

Julia and I followed him upstairs. He reached Downing's door and knocked loudly. "Downing? Downing!" he called.

There was no reply. He knocked again. "Downing," I called. There was still no answer.

"He seemed fine when he went to bed last night," Julia said hesitantly.

"He wasn't fine!" I said sharply. "Papa, he's ill. We must get in there right now. Right now!"

The color drained from Julia's face as a certain thought occurred to her. "He can't be that ill," she said feebly.

"Wait here," said Papa. He went into his own room.

"I'm scared, Edwina," whispered Julia. I put my arm around her. My heart was pounding madly. I should never have left him alone last night, I thought. Never, never, never!

Papa emerged from his room accompanied by his valet, a husky young fellow who had been assigned to him by the German tour manager. Although the young man spoke only broken English, Papa had apparently succeeded in making the problem clear to him, for he went straight to Downing's door. Lifting a foot, he took aim and gave the lock area one deft, powerful kick. There was a sound of splintering wood as the door sprang open.

Not until I smelled the clean air did I admit to myself I'd been terrified that when the door opened we would be greeted by the smell of gas. In relief, I rushed inside. "Wait, daughter," I heard Papa say, but I ignored him.

Downing lay in bed, the covers pulled up to his chin. "Downing?" I said softly as I approached. His head shifted slightly. I stood at the foot of the bed and looked down at him. He was awake, but he did not look up at me. "Downing? Are you all right?" I asked. He blinked but did not reply.

Papa and Julia came over to the bed. "Are you ill?" asked Papa.

Again Downing's eyelids fluttered. In a barely audible voice, he whispered two words: "I can't."

"What did he say?" asked Julia.

Someplace, somewhere, it seemed that something was severing. " 'I can't,' " I repeated dully. "He said, 'I can't.' "

Julia was bewildered. "Can't? Can't what, Downing?"

Very softly Downing groaned. With a seemingly monumental effort he turned his face to the wall. Julia sobbed.

He can't, I thought numbly. It's too late.

The valet had lingered by the door. "A doctor," Papa said to him. "One who speaks English." He pressed some bills into the young man's hand. "Edwina, please tell him we do not want the newspapers to know of this." Mechanically, I translated. The valet nodded and left.

I looked at the broken door. "I should never have left him alone," I said.

Dr. Leyden, a specialist in troubles of the nerves, examined Downing that afternoon. Dr. Leyden's reputation was of the highest caliber, and he was internationally known and respected. New patients frequently had to wait months for a consultation. Fortunately, Dr. Leyden was also a lover of Shakespeare. He was delighted to rearrange his schedule to be of service to the great tragedian Edwin Booth.

His prognosis was not good. It would be at least half a year until we could hope to see Downing in any semblance of good health. The accident in New York had possibly caused a deprivation of oxygen that damaged the brain. But if so, he said, it was odd that there had been recent improvements. It seemed to closely resemble other illnesses of the mind he had encountered.

To all of this I listened, but without response. There was nothing I could do.

Dr. Leyden prescribed stimulants that he said would energize Downing physically, but for the mental lethargy he could do nothing. He recommended a long rest in a sanitarium. Papa thanked him for coming. He promised him two tickets for that evening's performance of *Hamlet*, and two more for the opening of *Othello* later in the week.

Papa wrote to Calvert Vaux, who wrote back requesting that Downing return home. In two weeks Papa would go to Bremen to perform, and there Downing and Julia would board a ship for America. It was futile to protest. The last thing Downing needed in his current condition was to be dragged through a succession of foreign cities. The situation was out of my hands. I could only hope for the best.

On February 2 Downing and Julia departed on the liner *Donauo*. The weather was very cold, almost freezing, when the liner departed, yet I lingered, with Papa beside me on the pier, for a long time watching it go. After a while Papa said soothingly, "It's the best thing for him, daughter. Back in America he can receive the proper treatment."

"I know," I said hollowly.

"I have no doubt he'll be much better when we arrive home in the summer."

"Yes. He'll be better then."

"It's only a few months. The time will pass quickly."

"It will."

"And then you'll see him again, in New York."

I nodded. "Yes." I told myself I would see him then. He would greet me on the dock in New York, well on the road to recovery, perhaps even fully well. There was no reason to doubt it. Yet as I stood there on the Bremen pier I could not banish the awful feeling that I was never going to see him again.

At the end of the Berlin engagement, the citizens gave Papa a silver laurel wreath as a token of their high esteem. His great success was repeated in every city where he appeared. When his

Bremen engagement was through, he received a second wreath. There were other tributes in Hamburg and Hanover, and in Leipzig he received a third wreath. When the tour finally ended in April in Vienna, he received another.

Although each wreath was designed and inscribed differently, to me they all looked the same. Much of Germany had struck me that way also, a long procession of neat, tidy cities through which I had traveled with Papa on what had increasingly felt to me like a triumphal march. By the time we arrived in Vienna, I felt as though I had spent the previous two months sleepwalking, numb to the great crowds of admirers who mobbed us wherever we went. I had been barraged by new faces, places, and events, which now merged together into a single unit that endlessly repeated itself and was of no lasting significance to me at all, or to my life. My real life, I felt, had been temporarily suspended.

My ties to what I thought of as reality were my letters from home and the few American newspapers I could find. The newspapers were usually at least two weeks old, but I pored over them, clinging to any mention of people I knew. Letters I received were rewarding, and I tried not to dwell too much on the fact that I received none from Downing. He could hardly write letters while he was recuperating from such a serious illness, I told myself. I was glad he was not wasting his strength. I did receive letters from Julia, who seemed to feel he was getting well.

When the tour was finished we went to Paris for a short visit. While there I read in the American newspapers that Booth's Theatre had closed permanently at the end of April, having finally been sold for about half what it had cost to build. I almost cried when I read that it was to be changed into a dry goods store.

After Paris, we spent a month vacationing in England. I

would have preferred to return directly to America, but Papa said he needed a rest. England did seem a step closer to home, and it was a blessed relief to finally hear English spoken again. I felt that I was beginning to return to reality, awakening from a long sleep.

In June we departed from Liverpool for America on the liner *Gallia*, the same ship on which we had arrived the previous year. I was saddened by the reminder, since everything with Downing had been so different then, but fortunately our staterooms turned out to be in a completely different part of the ship.

The weather was good, and we made excellent time. As each day passed, my excitement increased at the thought of seeing Downing again. I told myself sternly that it was probable he was still not fully recovered. I had heard little of his progress. But wasn't it said that no news was good news? Ultimately, I could not resist hoping he would be on the dock waiting for me.

On the morning of the day we were to dock, while the ship was in quarantine in the harbor, Papa called me into his stateroom. "I've waited until the last possible moment to tell you this," he began, and I knew at once it was something about Downing.

"He will never fully recover," Papa continued somberly. Unknown to me, over the past few months Papa had received frequent reports of Downing's condition. These had not been good. He had shown almost no improvement, and the doctors now believed it would be years before he was well. "This is why I delayed a month in England," Papa explained. "I wanted to give him as much time as possible to show some signs of getting well. But he has not, and we can no longer avoid facing the inevitable. For your own sake, the engagement must be broken."

The engagement must be broken. Each word had the weight of a stone, a giant boulder rolling and crushing everything in its path. I must, I knew, make some effort at objection, however futile; I must display some sign that I would not meekly comply with this monstrous destruction. "No," I said in a small voice. "He needs me. He was starting to get well last winter when I was with him. But then I failed him. I should not have left him alone that night after the Berlin opening. He'd be well now if I hadn't."

"Daughter—"

I must have swayed a little, because Papa suddenly rushed to me and threw an arm around my shoulders. "Daughter," he said urgently, "be grateful we discovered this before you married him! The poor boy is deeply troubled. Surely you can see why this engagement must be broken."

All the feelings of hopelessness that I had managed to stave off for the past months now rushed in upon me. I felt nothing but a deep, empty despair.

"We'll go directly to our new house in Newport," I heard Papa telling me. His arm around my shoulder felt like a mantle of lead. "Fortunately, it has no memories for you, even though Calvert built it. We'll spend the summer resting. Grandma and Aunt Rosalie will come and stay with us."

I was never sure at what point I stopped listening. I did hear him say one thing further: "Of course, in a few days, if you like, you can write Downing a little note, telling him yourself. But he has already been told, so if you'd prefer not to, there is no need." I stumbled out and back into my stateroom.

Betty was waiting there. "Missy," she said, and I could tell from her tone that she already knew.

"I need air, Betty," I said hoarsely. "I'm going up on deck." I grabbed my bonnet and ran out.

On the promenade deck I leaned on the rail and breathed deeply. Don't think, don't think, not now, I told myself. If you think about it, you're going to cry. Somehow I held back the tears.

A few minutes later Betty came out looking for me. "Your papa wants you, missy. Some reporters for the newspapers came out to the ship to ask him about your trip. He wants you to sit with him."

I said nothing. I continued to stare out over the harbor at Brooklyn.

After a minute, Betty said quietly, "It's just not meant to be, missy. Now, you go down to the lounge and sit nice and polite next to your father while he talks to those reporters. Remember who you are, missy."

I gave a short, harsh laugh. "Of course, Betty. I am none other than Edwin Booth's daughter." I turned and went inside, then down to the lounge where Papa was surrounded by reporters.

"Here is my daughter, gentlemen," he said when he saw me. "She was the greatest help to me on this trip. Her command of the German language is excellent, you know."

"Say something in German for us, Miss Booth," called one of the reporters.

"I'm sorry," I said hollowly. "I've forgotten everything."

Hours later we disembarked and passed through customs. Then we separated; Betty and I went straight to Grand Central Depot for our train to Newport while Papa went downtown to visit his attorney and his banker. He would follow us on the next train.

The driver of our carriage chose Sixth Avenue for the long trip up to Grand Central. When we arrived at Twenty-third Street, I glanced out at Booth's Theatre. As I had feared, work had already begun, and much of the decorative outer façade had been stripped away. Soon everything that had made the building so special would be destroyed. Starting to cry, I turned away from the window.

On the train to Newport, I wrote to him.

> *Dearest Downing,*
>
> *I understand your illness too well to believe that anything I write will at present hold significance for you. Someday, sometime in years ahead, you will be well, at which time you will perhaps look back and wonder. It is for that time I now write that our parting occurs only with the deepest sadness and regret on my part. Even though I would still wish it otherwise, I somehow now believe our life together was not meant to be. Why, I do not understand, but I see it is the truth. We must follow it.*
>
> *Be well. Please, be well.*
>
> *Dearest Downing, good-bye.*
>
> *Edwina*

FIVE

1883

Vivid July sunlight surrounded me as I walked across the open field that lay between the house and the Seaconnet River. I had taken off my bonnet and unpinned my hair. Our property was private, so there was no chance that someone would come on me in such an improper hatless condition, and the boats that passed in the river were far enough away to render me indiscernible.

I had not realized how warm the afternoon was until I left the river with its cool water and breeze and began the trip across the field to the house—Boothden, as Papa had named it. I noted with indifference that although the sky overhead was cloudless, far away on the horizon tiny dark clouds were starting to appear. I wondered if it was going to rain.

Inside the house, I found Papa in the center hall. His hair was disheveled from his nap.

"Have a nice walk?" he asked.

"Yes."

"Good." He went to a window. "Some clouds are rolling in. We may have rain. I hope it holds off until Adam arrives."

His friend Adam Badeau was coming to stay for a few days. He was due to arrive that afternoon.

"Are things in order for him?" asked Papa.

I nodded. "We're putting him in the large front bedroom." The room, I added silently, that should have been Downing's.

Downing. At the thought of him, a wave of sadness rippled up inside me. I pushed the thought away. This was something I had learned to do.

On his way to Boothden to visit us that summer, General Badeau was stopping off to see his old colleague and benefactor General Grant. "To propose an idea," he had written mysteriously to Papa.

General Badeau had received international recognition for his multivolume *Military History of Ulysses S. Grant.* "Adam is an interesting, intelligent man," Papa told me, and from General Badeau's conversation at dinner on his first evening with us, I could see that this was true.

The steady patter of raindrops on the roof of the verandah provided a soothing backdrop to General Badeau's voice throughout the meal. That voice seldom stopped; the conversation at times approached a monologue. Papa was unusually silent with his erudite, extremely vocal friend.

The conversation outlasted the meal, and after dessert was finished we continued to sit at the table. Papa brought out a new bottle of brandy and poured some for the General and himself. Then Papa asked quietly, "And how was General Grant?"

"Fine, fine," General Badeau replied, a little too quickly. "Quite enjoying life as a private citizen." He then began to speak of something else. I had hoped to hear more of the mysterious proposal for General Grant about which he had written. From the abrupt way he changed the subject, however, I assumed he had been disappointed and did not wish to speak of it. I hoped Papa would not embarrass his friend by pursuing it further.

General Badeau began to complain about New York City.

"It really is becoming impossible," he said, his voice sounding very precise. "I look forward to each visit, and then I'm disappointed. It's so different from the New York of my youth. Now it's dirty, noisy, and so commercial. Barbarians are overrunning it. And to think they're turning your beautiful theatre into a dry goods store! It's enough to make one weep. Such a noble attempt to bring culture to the people, all come to naught."

The expression on Papa's face did not alter at the mention of Booth's Theatre. "Yes, it is sad," he said. "Now, tell me, Adam, what of your proposal to General Grant? It was successful, I trust?"

I was shocked to hear him ask this. Apparently he completely missed seeing that his friend did not want to speak of it. Papa was normally so perceptive! How could he have failed to notice? I glanced at his half-empty brandy glass. Although General Badeau's glass had been refilled, Papa had not even finished his first. Perhaps that small amount had been enough to dull his perception.

General Badeau did not respond to the question at once. His stout body seemed to swell a little, and he tugged nervously at one end of his waxed mustache. "No, it was not successful," he finally said in a voice laden with frustration. "My idea was for General Grant to collaborate with me in writing his autobiography. But he was not interested. He said that in the *Military History* I had already said everything that needed to be said. I tried to explain what a different thing this would be, but he couldn't see himself doing it. 'I'm too old to try something new now,' he told me. 'I wouldn't know how to.'" General Badeau sighed, clearly exasperated. It was evident that the conversation with General Grant had been extremely difficult for him. "Silly answers, really. He just didn't want to do it."

"It *is* a good idea," Papa said thoughtfully. "Did he understand how lucrative it would be?"

Overt sullenness appeared on the General's face. "Finances, my friend, are no longer a concern to him. His son's firm, Grant and Ward, has done spectacularly well, and the General has become a fourth partner. He will soon be a very rich man."

The night at Booth's Theatre when the Grants had appeared in the box opposite mine, Buck had looked happy and serene and comfortable with life. How proud it must make him to be the means by which his famous father could achieve financial security.

"Well, don't be too disappointed," Papa told him. "He may change his mind."

"No, no, no," General Badeau replied. "You don't know General Grant. Once he decides something, he never changes his mind—never, never, never. But I'm not criticizing him, you understand; this very quality made him a great general."

The steady rain suddenly increased to a downpour. Torrents of rain spattered against the roof and walls of the house. I stood up. "If you'll excuse me, I must check the windows upstairs." Papa and General Badeau stood and waited as I left the room.

Upstairs, everything was dry, and I thought I should return to the dining room. But I did not wish to, so I decided I would send down a message that I had retired early.

In the morning when I went down to breakfast, Betty told me Papa was still in his room, but General Badeau had breakfasted an hour earlier.

While I was sitting by myself at the table, a breeze stirred the blue curtains at the windows, drawing my attention to them. For the first time it struck me that their color was an awkward match to the wallpaper. They would have to be changed. Glancing around the room, I noticed other things that required attention. For the past month I had been living the life of a sleep-walker, barely aware of my surroundings—and in a new house, with so much to attend to!

The breeze from the window smelled so refreshing that I went to finish my coffee on the verandah. I found General Badeau sitting in one of the wicker chairs, reading the news-paper. "Good morning," I said.

"Good morning."

There was an awkward silence. I asked if he would like another cup of coffee. He replied that he would indeed, and I hurried inside to fetch it.

"Thank you so much," he said when I returned with it.

"I do want to apologize for vanishing so rudely last night."

"Think nothing of it. Your father and I were reminiscing. You would only have been bored, I fear."

"I always enjoy hearing about Papa's early days."

He sipped his coffee. "Your father's one of the few friends I have left from the days before the war. So many lost their lives during it."

"Papa told me you were wounded."

He looked up at me, evidently surprised that I knew this. I hoped I had not said the wrong thing; I only mentioned it in an attempt to make conversation.

But then he smiled, and I saw he was rather proud of the incident. "Why, yes, I was wounded, somewhat seriously. At the Battle of Port Hudson in Louisiana. I was shot in my left foot. Afterward I returned to New York and stayed at your father's house while I recuperated. Your father and your uncle both helped me to recover there."

"My uncle Joseph?"

"Oh, no. John Wilkes."

John Wilkes Booth. My body tensed the way it always did when The Subject was raised. A lifetime of habit responded, and at once I tried to think of a way to redirect the conversation. Of necessity I had grown very good at doing that.

But this time nothing would come. Shocked and confused, I glanced away from General Badeau's smiling face to the Seaconnet River in the distance.

Then I looked back at him, directly. The opportunity for me to finally learn more of my uncle was presenting itself. A year ago I would never have had the courage or even the inclination to do so. But harsh things had happened to me since then; perhaps I had earned the right to ask harsh questions. "Can you tell me what he was like?"

"Your uncle? A difficult question, to be sure. As an actor, he was enormously talented. It's highly possible his talent would have surpassed Edwin's, had he lived." General Badeau leaned back in his chair. "Personally, though, I'm uncertain anyone really knew him. He was handsome, with jet-black hair and blue eyes, a fair complexion. In manner, he was kind and gentle, yet strong. While I was recuperating at your father's house, it was John Wilkes who insisted on becoming my primary nurse. He was very gentle, troubled that I might be in pain."

The image of the man described was dramatically inconsistent with how one would imagine an assassin. I had expected to hear of extravagance and wild behavior. Could a kind and gentle man become an assassin? In a low voice, almost to myself, I asked, "Why did he do it?"

The General blinked nervously. "Pardon?"

Having started, I would continue. "I asked why my uncle assassinated Mr. Lincoln."

He shifted his weight in the chair and sat up very straight. Several seconds passed before he said, "Different people believe different things."

"Such as?"

"Well, your father believes that your uncle acted for the Knights of the Golden Circle."

"What?" I whispered, gaping at him.

"Your father believes that the Knights plotted President Lincoln's assassination and manipulated your uncle into carrying out their plans."

"There was a group behind him?"

He cleared his throat. "I said it was what your father believes. I did not say it was the truth."

"Is it?"

"Some people believe so," he answered evasively.

"But you do not?"

He stared into the distance, down toward the river. Clearly he was uncomfortable with the question.

I pulled up a chair and sat down close to him. "General," I said confidingly, "of course I would never dream of repeating to Papa anything you say. But you understand, he never talks of this, and I know so little about it. Please, tell me more about this group."

He sighed. "It's really not my place."

"Please."

He sat up very straight in his chair. When he spoke, his voice was low. "The Knights were a secret organization dedicated to stopping the Civil War. Their main goal was to eliminate the Republican government and make peace with the South."

"They favored the Confederacy?"

"It would be more accurate to say they favored the rights of the states instead of the federal government. That was why eventually in the North they came to be viewed with suspicion. Shortly before the end of the war many of the leaders were arrested, and the entire organization broke down. It had nearly disappeared by the time Lincoln was assassinated. Which, you see, is the main reason why I believe John Wilkes acted alone. The Knights were too weak by then to have planned it."

"Yes, I see."

"The Knights were pacifists. I doubt they would have endorsed assassination."

"But why does Papa believe it?"

"At first many people did. It came out that your uncle had been a member. But it was probably a coincidence."

"Wasn't there an investigation?"

"There was. They found nothing." He paused. "Edwin believes the plot was covered up. He believes people in high places were protected."

"But you do not?"

"No."

There was finality in his reply, but having come so far I would not retreat. "Then why did my uncle do it?"

"I think he was unhappy."

I recalled Downing's words about John Wilkes Booth: *They say he was mad.* "How unhappy?" I asked slowly. "Could it have been madness?"

For a long moment General Badeau was silent. "Madness?" he finally replied. "No, I do not think so. His manner was never unusual. I never even saw him sad." He paused. "But now, you make me consider. John Wilkes was lively and outgoing around everyone except Edwin—pardon, I mean your father. Around him he would often become quiet and subdued. It was rather odd. He would almost become smaller when your father was in the room."

I thought of the time Mama met Ellen Terry in London. She had become overwhelmed, deflated.

"But why?" I whispered.

"Who knows? As I said before, I think the man was very hard to know." He stood up. "Well! I think I'll take my constitutional now, down to the river and back." He asked if I would care to join him, but I politely declined. He clearly wanted to move on from our uncomfortable conversation.

That my uncle may have been involved in a plot was fascinating. The possibility that there were others who bore an equal measure of responsibility for the assassination, perhaps even a greater share of it, was very attractive to me. If so, it was extremely unfair that the full burden of blame had been placed on the shoulders of the Booth family. How splendid it would be if it one day turned out that Papa was right and General Badeau was wrong! And for all his convincing arguments, perhaps he *was* wrong. Unfortunately I could not question Papa about it.

As I sat on the porch my thoughts returned to the story of how John Wilkes Booth seemed to grow smaller around his brother Edwin. After a while I could not remember if in his description the General had used the word *smaller* or *crushed*.

Several days after General Badeau left, I woke up one night very thirsty. I had a powerful desire for cold water. I got up and went downstairs to the kitchen, where I poured a glass from the small bottle of water in the icebox. On my way back through the hall I noticed that the doors to the verandah were open. When I went to close them, I saw Papa sitting by himself on the steps leading down to the lawn. I stepped outside. "Papa?"

He turned toward me a little. I saw he was smoking one of his cigars. "Papa, why are you out here alone? In the dark?"

He inhaled deeply on the cigar. For a moment he said nothing but gazed up at the sky. I looked up too. Here and there tiny white stars were visible.

"Alone," he said softly. "Do you think, daughter, I will die alone?"

I shivered, from both the chill air and the question. "No, Papa. Certainly not. You have a family, and friends."

"My father had a wife and seven children. Yet he died alone."

"You mustn't think such foolish things," I said firmly. I went to him and kissed his head lightly. Then I went back inside.

At the end of July, Papa and I received an invitation to a luncheon-picnic at the nearby home of Julia Ward Howe. Although I had never met her, she and Papa had been friends for a long time. "Your mother and she were close," Papa told me. "She was even present at her funeral." Mrs. Howe's life was as full as Papa's, and they had not seen much of each other for the past two decades. When she discovered we lived but a few miles from her, she issued an invitation at once. "There'll be a crowd, and we won't have much of a chance to catch up, but *do* come," she had written.

The only thing I knew of Mrs. Howe was that during the war she had written "The Battle Hymn of the Republic," a famous poem I did not particularly care for. The Lord presented in it struck me as violent and unpleasant, with none of the qualities of mercy and forgiveness I had heard so much about at St. Mary's. Indeed, I once wondered if the sisters at St.

Mary's, mostly gentle, kind women, would have recognized Mrs. Howe's trampling and terrible Lord. More likely they would have thought him the devil.

Papa told me more about Mrs. Howe as we rode in our buggy to her house, Oak Glen, on the afternoon of the luncheon. "In addition to being a poetess of the first order, she has dedicated her life to social reform. Her husband was one of America's foremost abolitionists, and she assisted him greatly with his work. Unfortunately, in recent years she's become involved in this suffrage nonsense. I suspect we may have to humor her this afternoon."

The National Woman's Suffrage Association had been founded by Susan B. Anthony and Elizabeth Cady Stanton. I knew little about it, except that these women had been insistent that women be given the right to vote.

I felt ambivalent about being able to vote. I had never been interested in politics, but I disliked the fact that that those who believed in women's right to vote were frequently ridiculed, held up to scorn. Papa's remark about humoring Mrs. Howe on the subject bothered me. Making fun of someone's beliefs seemed to me as bad as ridiculing a person's religion. I never voiced these opinions, both because I knew Papa wouldn't agree and because I didn't feel strongly about them, but I was fascinated to learn that Mrs. Howe was an advocate of women's suffrage and a social reformer. As we drove up to her house I fully expected to meet a virtual Amazon of a woman, someone along the lines of Ellen Terry.

I could not have been more surprised by the conventional-looking, sweet-faced woman who came out to greet us as we pulled up to Oak Glen. She was primly dressed, her gray hair neatly parted in the middle. She reminded me more of Grandma

Booth than anyone else, although Mrs. Howe looked much younger, perhaps in her late sixties.

"*Young Hamlet, with his forehead grief subdued, and visionary eye,*" she recited in a soft voice.

Papa looked embarrassed. "Perhaps it should be *old* Hamlet now, my dear Julia. After all, you wrote that poem about me way back in 1858."

He introduced me. "How like your mother you are," Mrs. Howe said matter-of-factly.

We walked around to the side of the house. Oak Glen was as regular in appearance as Mrs. Howe. The house itself resembled a giant barn. "Dr. Howe bought this as our summer home thirty years ago," she told us. "I disliked it at first, but I've come to love it." She tapped Papa's arm. "I wrote your play here. Your ill-fated Greek tragedy. Does Edwina know of it?"

"No, no," Papa said. Again he looked embarrassed.

"Right after I met your father I sat down and wrote a play for him, an adaptation of *Hippolytus* by Euripides. And what luck I had! He and Charlotte Cushman chose to play it, at the Athenaeum in Boston. We were all set to begin when the manager suddenly decided not to do it. He did not even offer a satisfactory excuse! I was devastated, of course."

"How unfortunate," I said. I glanced at Papa. He was trying not to laugh.

We rounded the corner of the house. On a lawn halfway between us and the edge of a forest, a long table had been set up, ready for a formal luncheon. It looked completely out of place in the center of the open lawn, as though the walls and floor around it had been blown away. "I do hope the rain holds off," Mrs. Howe said, which struck me as odd, for there wasn't a cloud in the sky.

A group of elegantly dressed ladies and gentlemen were

seated on straight-back chairs near the table, drinking wine from crystal goblets. "We've quite a crowd for lunch today, twenty guests," said Mrs. Howe. We paused for a moment by the corner of the house. "Not just the old-timers today, either. Some of the new-money people are here." Her hands fluttered in a gesture of futility. "We can't completely ignore them, you know. They seem to have taken over Newport. Some of them are actually quite bright and intellectually inclined. Come, let me introduce you." She linked one arm through Papa's and the other through mine, and steered us across the lawn.

Luncheon was unpleasant. The sun was in my eyes for most of the meal, and a wasp kept buzzing around my head. Several heavily perspiring servants rushed back and forth to the house with dishes; cold foods were warm and warm foods were cold by the time they reached the table. The conversation was interesting, though. Mrs. Howe spoke about her involvement the previous year in organizing the first Women's Department at an industrial fair in Boston. The exhibit had shown how women contribute to society, especially through science and trade. It had been a great success, and received much notice and attention. "And," Mrs. Howe said, "I've been invited to organize a similar exhibition at the World's Fair in New Orleans this fall."

When we finished eating, Mrs. Howe led us down into the forest to show us what she called her salon. Although it did feel a bit odd for twenty well-dressed people to be marching off into a forest, the shade was a welcome relief from the sunlight that had beaten down on us during luncheon. "It reminds me of *As You Like It*," I whispered to Papa. I was surprised to see how relaxed and comfortable he appeared as we strolled along under the trees. I was reminded that he had spent the early years of his life in rural Maryland.

The salon was a small brookside glen, which was obviously tended in the manner of a small garden. Carpet-like green sod covered the ground, and the branches of several tall oak trees formed a canopy. The sound of the gently rippling brook was hypnotic.

"My children and I have spent much time in this wonderful place," Mrs. Howe said sentimentally. For some reason, the fact that she had children took me by surprise. Papa hadn't mentioned motherhood when listing her many accomplishments, and I simply assumed she had not had time for raising children. Now, Papa whispered to me that she had several daughters.

The luncheon ended soon after the visit to the salon, and we left. Papa looked a little tired, and I offered to drive. I was perfectly capable of handling the one-horse buggy. But Papa refused to let me. "Soon you'll be wanting a bicycle," he muttered. After a few minutes I was glad he had chosen to drive. I relaxed back in the seat. The air of the country lane was sweet with the smell of clover and honeysuckle.

"What a shame about that play she wrote for you," I said when my drifting thoughts arrived at it. "Why do you suppose the manager canceled it?"

"Because I asked him to."

I sat up and stared at him. He grinned mischievously. "Dear Mrs. Howe became somewhat carried away writing that play," he said. "When I read the finished draft, I was extremely embarrassed. Since I couldn't very well tell her I didn't like it, I arranged with the manager to have it canceled. That way, her feelings were spared."

He shook the reins, bringing the horse up to a trot. "Edwina, Mrs. Howe is an exceptional woman, there is no question. But some of her opinions are extreme and must not be taken too seriously. Allowances must be made for eccentricity in those of great talent. You must learn to disregard that which is simply eccentric."

"Yes, Papa." Once again I leaned back in the seat. He was referring mainly to her views on women's suffrage. But I was intrigued by what Mrs. Howe had told us of the women's exhibit. When one stopped to think about it, women did make great contributions to society. Some were scientists, some inventors. I supposed that if one truly had an exceptional ability it would find expression. I myself had no exceptional talent that would enable me to participate in such an exhibition. But I could not deny that I was still interested in viewing one.

In the fall, Papa bought another house, number Twenty-nine Chestnut Street on Beacon Hill in Boston. Whereas Boothden was a modern house full of sharp angles and vivid contrasts, the house on Chestnut Street was all curves and flowing lines.

We moved in during the first week of October. Most of the furnishings had been purchased along with the house, and Papa arranged for the many other things he had placed in storage over the years to be sent to his new home. Crate upon crate of furnishings, books, artwork, and mementos were waiting to be unpacked when we arrived. After exploring the house and selecting our bedrooms, we set to work unpacking in the dining room. Papa chatted happily as each item was removed and unwrapped. Each one had a bit of his personal history attached to it. Fortunately, none of these items were from his darker days, and his spirits remained high. Over and over he remarked how wonderful it felt to finally have a home for all his treasures. "And now I can grow old surrounded by the things that have made my life worthwhile," he said at one point.

"Papa, you're far from old," I said reassuringly.

Dinner was served early, and I was pleased with the quality of the food and the service. With the exception of Betty, all the servants were new, recommended by friends of Papa's in Boston. I introduced myself when we first arrived and briefly discussed menus with the housekeeper; then I decided I would simply observe for several days and make whatever changes were necessary afterward.

We were just finishing dinner when Papa's lawyer arrived to attend to some details having to do with the purchase of the house. Papa took him into his study, and I told the maid to bring them coffee. Glad to have some time alone, I went upstairs to begin making myself familiar with my new bedroom.

The room had obviously been decorated for a woman, with flowered wallpaper, upholstery, and draperies in shades of pale rose and yellow. A soft carpet patterned with flowers covered the entire floor, and on top of this several small, intricately designed oriental throw rugs had been placed in strategic locations.

At twilight, I sat in the graceful armchair by the window, wondering about the previous occupant of the room, the one it had been decorated for. Gradually the light faded; Papa would be finishing with the lawyer and waiting for me. I got up and went out into the hallway to go downstairs. The servants had not yet turned on the gas lamps, so it was nearly dark in the hall.

When I reached the top of the stairs I stopped, hearing Papa and the lawyer in the vestibule below. Papa was just showing him out.

"Yes, I'm very pleased with the house," Papa was saying. "I'm sure we'll be comfortable here for a long while."

"And is your daughter equally pleased with it?" the lawyer asked.

"Very much so," Papa replied. "In fact, I have no doubt the two of us will be living here for many years."

The lawyer murmured some polite response and said goodbye. I heard the front door open and close as he left. Then I heard the sounds of Papa's footsteps as he returned to the study.

I stood in the dark hallway, rooted to the floor, my hands gripping the banister. *For many years.* That was what Papa had said. What had he meant? Did he believe I would remain with him here unmarried for the rest of my life?

A lump of ice formed in my chest. I felt nauseated and a little dizzy. I stumbled back through the hallway into my bedroom, closed the door, and stood alone in the center of the dark room.

For many years? Papa could not really believe that. Surely he understood that I would one day be marrying and leaving to live with my husband. Did he think that my broken engagement had forever ended my plans for a marriage?

Suddenly I knew that even if Papa would never say so openly, this was what he wanted. Nothing would please him more than for me to remain here, in this house, with him. He wanted me here as he grew old, the same way he wanted the things he had unpacked from the crates downstairs. I thought of doing this, living here for years, caring for him the way Aunt Rosalie cared for Grandma Booth. Soon I would become quiet and withdrawn. In a few years I would stop going outside, would seldom speak to anyone. I would sit all day in the parlor, looking out a window.

How dare Papa want that for me! A rush of deep anger and resentment swept through me. I was shocked; I had never before felt this way toward him. At once I felt guilty. Papa thought he was doing the best thing for me. He had probably been frightened to think I had almost married a man on the verge of a nervous breakdown. He most likely wanted to protect me.

I would have to explain to him that this was not the best thing for me—that even though I had been through a difficult experience, I still hoped to marry in the near future. Yes, I would definitely have to sit down and talk to him about this. The sooner the better, before the idea became too set in his mind. In fact, it would probably be best if I went down and told him right now.

I took a step toward the door, and stopped. What if he didn't understand? I told myself this was nonsense. Papa had never wanted anything for me but my happiness. He would never oppose the idea of my marrying, once he knew I wanted to.

My hand was just touching the doorknob when into my mind came the image of him as he had been on the steps of Boothden the night he had asked me if he would die alone.

For a moment I thought I was going to faint. My lungs seemed to have suddenly become paralyzed; I felt I was suffocating. Gasping for air, I staggered to the window and threw it open.

The cool fall air flooded in around me, and the iron grip on my lungs relaxed. For a long time I stood there, breathing.

In late October, Henry Irving and Ellen Terry arrived in New York for their first American tour. The entire Lyceum Company, with all the scenery and paraphernalia for six elaborate productions, had been brought also. Mr. Abbey, their manager as well as Papa's, had understood perfectly that Henry Irving's productions, rather than Henry Irving alone, would be the draw.

Papa and I were in Boston when they arrived, since Papa's first engagement that fall was to be at Boston's Globe Theatre. Knowing Mr. Irving's schedule, Papa had carefully planned his own season so as to avoid conflict. He would not appear in New York until December, when Mr. Irving would be gone.

As was typical for any Abbey enterprise, the New York arrival was accompanied by a great deal of fanfare and publicity, all of which was reported in the Boston newspapers. Countless stories appeared in which Mr. Irving was praised for his dignified bearing, Miss Terry for her charm and beauty. Scores of questions were put to them by reporters, including, at one point, what Mr. Irving thought of Mr. Booth. At once he replied that he believed Papa was a magnificent actor.

Two opening nights were held, one for each star without the other. Mr. Irving appeared first playing Mathias, the innkeeper slowly going mad from guilt in the play *The Bells*. Although it was pouring rain that night, the opening was attended by the best of New York society. Some newspapers reported that tickets for the evening had been impossible to obtain for weeks. The next morning the reviews were ecstatic, and that evening the success was repeated when Miss Terry opened as the queen in *Charles XI*. Once again, the reviewers were jubilant. Irving and Terry's modern style was called an artistic revelation. Great art had arrived in America.

Papa read all this without comment. His only remark was at one point to say quietly, "How surprising he doesn't offer more Shakespeare."

I wondered if his feelings were as ambivalent as my own. Of course we were greatly indebted to Mr. Irving, who had helped Papa's 1881 English season by presenting him in *Othello*. And there were those splendid comments he had made about Papa in his interview. Yet I could not help but feel resentful when I remembered the reception Papa had received when he had first opened in London. Far from clamoring to see him, the way Americans were now clamoring to see Mr. Irving, Londoners had for the most part ignored him. I soon realized that my resentment would more properly be directed toward my fellow countrymen, who made such ado over a foreigner.

If Papa was resentful, he never showed it. He went on placidly with his own work, opening at the Globe in mid-November. In early December we traveled to New York, where he was to open at the Star Theatre.

I did not care for this theatre at all. Unlike Booth's Theatre, which had been close to the elegant Madison Square, the Star Theatre was on Thirteenth Street and Union Square. Union Square was commercial and loud. At night the new electric lights were glaring. Worse, the theatre itself was disgraceful. The work areas were dark and cramped, the dressing rooms cold and dirty. Henry Irving and the Lyceum Company had left things in a state of disarray when they departed. That annoyed me more than it would have if it had been anyone else.

Papa opened in the title role of *Richelieu*. As expected, he was compared with Henry Irving. Although his own performance did not fare so badly with the critics, some preferring his natural style to Mr. Irving's mannerisms, his supporting company and the presentation as a whole were severely criticized. Papa was also criticized for always offering the same pieces, unlike Mr. Irving, who tried new plays such as *The Bells*. A few reviewers—not many, but some—called him old-fashioned next to the modern Mr. Irving.

We were to stay in our usual suite at the Brunswick. Apprehensive about the many sad memories I associated with the hotel, both of Downing and of Mama, I hinted that I would prefer to stay at another. There were many fine hotels, such as the fashionable Brevoort House, closer to the Star Theatre. But Papa remarked that he much enjoyed the familiarity of the Brunswick suite, and I said nothing further. His comfort while performing was my primary concern.

During the first matinee performance, on a blustery cold Saturday afternoon, my errands brought me close to the theatre. This was not surprising, because the Star was located in the center of New York's main shopping area, Broadway between Twenty-third and Canal Streets. I decided that, being so nearby, I should visit Papa backstage during the performance.

I arrived a little before the second intermission, so I went to his dressing room to wait. As I sat down and unbuttoned my cloak, the door opened and old Henry Flohr wobbled in, carrying one of Papa's costumes. "Hello, Henry," I said.

Startled, he stared at me as if seeing a ghost. I guessed that I reminded him now, as I had before, of my mother. Finally he said, "Little Edwina! What a surprise!"

"Papa didn't tell me you were working for him here."

"Oh, yes, Miss Edwina. I haven't had much work since Booth's Theatre closed. I came to see Mr. Booth right away when he arrived in New York, and he took me on. And I'm to go on to Brooklyn, Baltimore, and Philadelphia with him too!" He carefully laid the costume down on a chair. "Mr. Booth is a good, good man, Miss Edwina. He never forgets anyone, always remembers his old friends, even when he'd do better with someone else."

"Papa always said you were the best dresser he ever had, Henry."

He chuckled a little. "God bless you, Miss Edwina, but I'm old now! Look at this." He came over to me, extending his hands. Even in the dim light of the dressing room I could see that the knuckles and joints were swollen and bent with rheu-matism. "Some days when it's cold they freeze right up on me. Those days, your papa could have a younger man who'd do the job in half the time. But he sticks with me. God bless your papa, Miss Edwina, God bless him!"

The sight of his hands disturbed me. I changed the subject. "Papa doesn't expect me here today."

"He'll be very pleased, yes he will! You just sit right there, and he'll be here in no time at all." He glanced at the dressing table. "I have things to set out for him, Miss Edwina, so you must excuse me for a while."

"Don't mind me, Henry. Please do what you have to do."

He went to the table and began to rearrange the makeup tins and brushes, difficult work for his hands. Suddenly I found myself wondering how many other tired, worn hands had served Papa.

At the dressing table, Henry began to hum to himself. What would Henry think if I told him everything I was lately thinking about Papa? How I was wondering about his behavior with his friends? With General Badeau, for instance, when Papa had insisted on speaking of a subject he clearly had not wanted to discuss? Or about his attitude toward Mrs. Howe? What would Henry, who thought the world of Papa, do? He would stare at me, aghast. He would certainly never believe a word of it. It was unbelievable, of course. My imagination was working overtime. Papa was good and kind and helped everyone.

Then I thought of the way he had behaved the day he first met Downing. He had told the story about Downing refusing to paint the picture at his uncle's house when he was a little boy. Downing suspected he had deliberately told it differently from how it had actually been. At the time I thought Papa hadn't wished to embarrass him. Now I knew otherwise. Papa's motives had been much less pleasant. He had wanted to test Downing to see if he would disagree with him.

Suddenly I knew I absolutely could not see Papa right now. A heavy throbbing was starting at my temples. If I hurried, I could get away before he arrived in the dressing room. I stood up. "Henry," I said, "I just remembered I have to go someplace right now. But please, say nothing to Papa about my having been here. Nothing at all!"

He tottered over to me. His feet, I now realized, were probably as cramped and gnarled as his hands. "Not a word, not a word," he said. "But, Miss Edwina, let me get you a carriage."

"There's no time!" I ran out of the dressing room.

I stumbled downstairs and out the stage door without encountering anyone. Outside, a blast of near-arctic wind reminded me my cloak was still open. I buttoned it hastily as I raced down the alley next to the theatre toward Broadway.

It's true! It's true! a little voice screeched in my head, whipping me on as if I were being chased. I had a terrible urge to run, to hurry, to rush away somewhere. My heart pounded madly. I had no destination, no goal other than to keep moving.

Reaching Broadway, I turned right, heading downtown. Despite the frigid temperature, the street was crowded with Christmas shoppers, all carefully making their way along the slippery sidewalk. Patches of ice were brightly visible in many places, and the accumulation of snow from recent snowfalls glared in the brilliant afternoon sun. For all its brightness, the sun provided no warmth this afternoon.

Icy wind stung my face as I rushed along. My single thought was to keep moving. Approaching the corner of Twelfth Street, I ran directly onto a patch of ice. An instant later I was sprawled on my side in the street, looking up into the oncoming stomping legs of a pair of horses. "No!" I cried aloud, and pulled myself up onto my knees. The carriage veered to the right, whisking past me.

Two men rushed forward to help me. "I'm fine, I'm fine," I said in answer to their worried inquiries. A pile of soft snow had cushioned my fall, and I hadn't been hurt. I thanked the men and continued down Broadway, but slowly now, avoiding the ice. But far from slowing, my inner state of agitation only increased.

My face was numb from the cold. Looking up, I saw a massive iron and glass building. I had come directly to A. T. Stewart's department store, one of the places I had intended to shop that afternoon. I needed to buy some lace handkerchiefs, a Christmas gift from Papa to his mother, and Stewart's had wonderful imported lace. Perhaps if I pulled myself together, exerted my will, and put my mind to a simple task, I would shake the wretched thoughts that were now clawing at me.

The immense plate-glass windows of the store around the Broadway entrance were decorated for Christmas, but I barely noticed them as I rushed along and joined the crowd streaming into the store. Inside, it was packed with a mob of noisy, jostling shoppers. Although the warmth was a welcome relief, I got no farther than the great central rotunda before I could no longer stand to be in such close proximity to so many human beings. The lace would have to wait for another day. Feeling as though I was going to faint, I pushed my way to the exit.

Back on Broadway, I continued a few blocks farther downtown. The shops became smaller, less imposing than the monolithic Stewart's. The windows of one store, brightly decorated, caught my eye. The store was crammed with toys of all types:

dolls, rocking horses, toy soldiers, and stuffed animals. I stopped and stared. One of the dolls was the same as one I had owned when I was a little girl. Suddenly I was seized with a desire to go into the store, to surround myself with childhood toys, to play and forget I had ever grown up at all.

Inside, the store was much less crowded than Stewart's. The warmth felt good, and for a moment I simply stood still just inside the entrance. The front-door clerk, an elderly man with a thin face, came over and inquired what I wished to purchase. Purchase? I stared at him. Could he not see I was too old to play with toys? "Nothing for myself," I answered.

"Something for your children?" he asked politely. "For a boy or a girl?"

"No," I said stupidly. "I have no children."

His expression changed, his eyes narrowed. He thinks me odd, I thought. I should say something, offer any silly lie as to why I had come into the store. But nothing would come.

The clerk was just starting to speak again when a clear, deep voice rang out. "Why, Miss Booth! What a pleasant surprise!" I turned and saw Mr. Ignatius Grossmann, smiling widely.

The clerk politely stepped away. Mr. Grossmann was carrying several parcels. "I've been shopping for gifts for my nieces and nephews," he said, "although I must confess I myself enjoy spending time here. It's almost the same as being a child again."

"Yes," I whispered. I glanced up at him just in time to see the realization dawn in his eyes that I was terribly upset. "Miss Booth," he asked quietly, "is something wrong?"

There, in the middle of the children's toy store on lower Broadway, I started to cry.

————

Mr. Grossmann took me to a nearby Beer Garden. There were several in the city, serving New York's many upright, respectable German immigrants. "Although I'm Hungarian, not German, I've always been at home in the Gardens," he told me as we went in. He asked if I was hungry. When I said no, he steered me to one of the tables. As soon as I was comfortably seated, he dashed off into the nearby bar room for refreshments.

Alone, I looked around. Everything was unpretentious. A mural was painted on the ceiling, but beyond that the hall was undecorated except for holiday wreaths and branches of pine on the walls. For all its lack of elegance, the hall was enormously inviting and appealing. I was glad we had come here rather than to some small, crowded restaurant.

He returned with two beverages, a glass mug of dark, foaming beer for himself and a smaller glass of wine for me. "A Rhine wine, excellent vintage," he said as he placed it before me. He sat down across from me and took a drink of his beer.

I sipped my wine; it tasted light and satisfying. I said, "I traveled all over Germany but never went to a place as comfortable as this. Thank you for bringing me here."

"I knew it wouldn't be crowded at this hour. Tonight it will be packed, until very late. There'll be lots of noise, laughter, good music, and singing, but with no disorderliness or rowdy behavior." He drank some more of his beer. "I like the atmosphere. I take most of my meals here."

"It is pleasant." I had been chilled when we came in, but now, feeling warm, I reached to undo my cloak. I had buttoned it all unevenly. I had walked all the way from the Star Theatre with it that way. I had probably been stared at all the way down Broadway! I glanced up at Mr. Grossmann, hoping he hadn't noticed. As usual, he was smiling; or was it his wide mustache that gave his face its always-cheerful expression? But no, he was smiling now, in a way that looked understanding, not mocking. I had no doubt that he had noticed the unevenly buttoned cloak the moment he saw me in the toy store. I sighed. "The clerk must have thought me a lunatic."

"You were upset."

"Thank you for being there when I needed someone."

"An honor to be of help."

I saw he had no intention of prying into the reason that had brought me to that condition; he was too much of a gentleman for that. Although I felt no pressure to explain, I did feel a peculiar desire to speak to him. In fact, I felt a strong urge to begin blurting out everything about Papa, all the horrid things I was thinking about him. Of course, I could not.

"This city has sad reminders for me," I said. "My stepmother died here."

"Yes. I'm sorry."

"And my fiancé lived here. But our engagement had to be broken."

"I'm sorry. I hadn't heard that. But I had heard that Mr. Vaux became ill after an accident."

"It wasn't an accident. He tried to kill himself."

There it was; I had finally said it out loud. I could no longer remember when I came to admit it to myself, even though I now believed some part of me knew it from the first.

Mr. Grossmann's smile faded. But my shocking announcement had not revolted or frightened him, or caused him to retreat from me. His eyes were full of gentle sympathy. "I'm so sorry," he said softly.

I took a drink of my wine. "Yes, that's what it was, an attempt at suicide, although no one will admit it. It's easier for them to call it an accident. Maybe they truly believe it was. None of them understood Downing in the least. Not even I." Having finally broken the initial barrier to the subject by speaking aloud, the rest was easier to talk of. "At first I blamed myself, thinking that if I had married him sooner it wouldn't have happened. But it would have made no difference. He was greatly troubled, had been so for years. He was trying to be an artist. As it turned out, though, he didn't want to be one at all."

"Yes, I remember you once told me you wanted to be the wife of an artist."

"I still do."

"Forgive me, but why? I must confess I didn't understand your reasons then. I still don't."

I looked at him, remembering. Yes, I had spoken to him on the night that he had accompanied me to Gramercy Park. "Well, there are many reasons," I said. But surprisingly, I couldn't think of any. My mind was blank when I tried to remember.

My face must have changed, for right away he apologized for asking. I could see from the small creases appearing in his wide, smooth forehead that he was genuinely distressed at having troubled me with his question.

"Lately I've been wondering if any of us really know why we do anything," I said, managing a smile.

A short while later he accompanied me back to the Brunswick. Leaving the carriage, I once again thanked him for treating me so kindly that afternoon. I offered him my hand to shake. He held it for a moment in both of his. "Miss Booth, it would please me enormously if you would consider me your friend."

"I already do, Mr. Grossmann," I said sincerely. His wide smile grew even wider.

Papa always stayed at the theatre between the matinee and evening performances, so he would not be back to the hotel until very late that night. If I were in bed by then, as I frequently was, I would not have to see him until the next morning. I was glad of this, for I was still deeply troubled by what I had realized at the theatre that afternoon. More immediately troubling to me was the question Mr. Grossmann had asked me that I had been unable to answer: Why had I always wanted to marry an artist?

The question recurred as I went into my bedroom and took off my hat. As though in response, into my thoughts came the image of a photograph my grandmother had in her house in Long Branch, a photograph of John Wilkes Booth.

In the morning, before I went in to breakfast, I had some minor qualms about actually seeing Papa. Suppose I became upset again when I looked at him? What if he sensed that I was different, that there had been some irrevocable change in my attitude toward him? Would his brown eyes become cold, staring at me accusingly?

But nothing unpleasant or difficult happened. He was the same as he'd always been, smiling fondly at me, offering me his cheek to kiss. I was relieved to discover that, in spite of everything I now knew, I loved him not one bit less. He was still Papa, my Papa.

"Do you remember Mr. Grossmann?" I asked toward the end of the meal. "Mr. Neville's brother. You met him backstage when Mr. Neville approached you about the Actor's Order a few years back."

He glanced up from his meal. "Yes. He has a German accent."

"It's Hungarian, actually. Or it was, I mean. The accent's gone now." I paused. "I ran into him yesterday while I was shopping. I had coffee with him." There was no reason to tell Papa I'd had wine.

He looked at me, surprised. "Did you now!"

"Yes. He's very nice."

"I'm sure he is. But still, I would not have expected it. He's a bit different from you, isn't he? He's a bookkeeper or something?"

"A stockbroker, Papa," I said gently.

"Oh, those business jobs are all the same to me."

"There's quite a difference between them."

"Well, I suppose there must be someone to do that work, mustn't there?" He smiled at me and turned back to his mail.

Without having said so, he had made it perfectly clear that he did not think very highly of Mr. Grossmann. I would not let this disturb me, for my potential friendship with him would be none of Papa's concern. Still, I found it annoying that Papa could so easily trivialize someone else's work.

Mr. Grossmann had mentioned the hotel at which he lived, and that afternoon I wrote him a short letter to thank him once again for his kindness. The next day a note came from him, stating that he hoped I would never hesitate to call on him for anything. Two days later I sent him a Christmas card, and later in the week I received one back from him. Our correspondence had begun, and after the holidays I would write to him again.

Grandma Booth and Aunt Rosalie arrived the week before Christmas for a stay of three days. Papa had written to them in July asking them to come live with us, but they replied firmly that their home was in Long Branch. Further, they declined even a visit, claiming that the long trip would be too strenuous and exhausting. For several days after receiving their reply Papa had been silent and withdrawn. Then he had written back, telling them they were always welcome if they should change their minds. I'd hoped they would, for I hadn't seen them in over a year, and I missed them. I felt better when I received a nice letter from Grandma Booth, saying that in the fall or early winter she would manage a trip to New York to see me. Papa, it seemed, had no intention of relenting on his refusal to let me visit the Long Branch house while Uncle Joe's new wife was there.

Papa took additional rooms for them near ours at the Brunswick. On the morning of their arrival we took the ferry to the Pennsylvania Railroad Station in Jersey City to meet their train. The large waiting room was very crowded, so we decided to stroll up and down the platform. Papa was strangely silent as we walked. When we reached a certain point he simply stopped and stared at the empty tracks over the edge.

"What is it, Papa?" I asked softly.

After a moment, in a voice distant and low, he said, "It was right here that in 1864 I saved a life."

"Really, Papa?" He had never told me this before, although we had been to this station countless times.

"Oh, yes." He said nothing further.

"What happened?" I prompted.

"A young fellow, part of the crowd, slipped and began to fall beneath the wheels of a moving train. I caught him and pulled him back to the platform."

"Oh, Papa! You saved his life!"

"That young man was Robert Lincoln, the son of the President."

A month ago I would have stared at him, mouth agape,

speechless with astonishment. But now my surprise was tempered by doubt.

Papa did not even seem to notice that I had not replied. He began to speak as though I had shrieked with surprise. "Yes, daughter, a most unbelievable coincidence. That winter morning I saved the life of Robert Lincoln, and little more than a year later occurred the"—he hesitated—"great tragedy."

"Did no one remember?" I asked cautiously.

"Eventually, yes. In fact, I was finally allowed to recover my brother's body some years later because of the incident." He said no more, and we strolled on. I wondered if this tale could be true. If so, it should be made widely known, for it certainly seemed in many ways to compensate for my uncle's crime, at least insofar as any responsibility borne by the rest of his family was concerned. Certainly people would view Papa differently if they knew of this. That it had been kept secret, when it could have been so enormously useful, caused me to doubt its credibility even more. I would definitely seek to verify it when the opportunity arose.

The train finally arrived and Grandma Booth emerged, looking as old and frail as she always looked. Aunt Rosalie, however, appeared more animated than usual. Her eyes were wide and bright as she looked around at the activity in the station, but I could not tell if this alertness was due to excitement or fear. With a flutter of resentment, I watched the way she doted on her mother, never straying far from her side, always ready to assist her or attend to her needs. Was this, I wondered, the future that Papa had begun to envision for me?

SIX

1884

It was inevitable that Papa's tour would eventually cross paths with Mr. Irving's. This occurred at the end of March, in New York, when Papa returned to the city to finish with a two-week engagement at the Fourteenth Street Theatre. At that same time Henry Irving was concluding his own tour with a return engagement at the Star Theatre, the final week of which overlapped with the first week of Papa's engagement. "It can't be helped," Papa said with a shrug when I questioned him about alternatives. "But he and I are not offering any of the same pieces, so I doubt there'll be any ill feeling."

Mr. Irving chose to open with Shakespeare's *Much Ado About Nothing*, with himself as Benedick and Miss Terry as Beatrice. He had not offered this play during his first engagement in New York the previous fall. The publicity surrounding this second opening rivaled that of the first, and once again the reviews were spectacular. Critics raved not only about the performances of the two stars but also about the stunning production, which included more than ten stage settings, the most magnificent of which was the reproduction of the cathedral at Messina. The implication was clear: the critics believed that Mr. Irving had surpassed Papa even in Papa's specialty, Shakespeare.

I doubted that they could be right. In *Othello* Mr. Irving had been at best Papa's equal, and the only other time I had seen him perform was in *The Cup*, a non-Shakespearean play. His acting talent had not impressed me in either play, although Miss Terry's had in both. It seemed that Mr. Irving, knowing his weakness, surrounded himself with superior talent to compensate for his inability to convey the emotional heart of a character. The spectacular staging of *Much Ado About Nothing* was probably intended to have the same effect. Could all the New York critics, the most sophisticated in the country, have failed to see this? Or was it true that he was better than Papa? I would have to go and find out for myself.

I went alone, quietly, to the midweek matinee performance when Papa had his own matinee. I wore a dark veil pinned down over my face, and purchased a seat in the rear mezzanine where it was unlikely I would be recognized. For three hours I sat nearly mesmerized, with the rest of the audience, as a work of dramatic art of near-perfect beauty in all its aspects unfolded before me on the stage. Mr. Irving did not have the natural talent of Papa, but Papa had never achieved the artistic heights of Mr. Irving. What Papa offered was a magnificent interpretation of one character, one man. What Mr. Irving offered was a magnificent interpretation of the panorama of life itself. Papa surpassed Mr. Irving as an actor, but Mr. Irving surpassed him with his artistic vision.

The vision of life Papa offered, the play as a whole, was often a little lopsided. Consistently, reviews of Papa's productions criticized the weakness of his supporting casts. This had been the case even at Booth's Theatre, where the settings were spectacular. Papa frequently had extremely bad luck in his choice of supporting players. It had always been a matter of one superb performance, surrounded by mediocrity.

At first I wondered how Papa could so consistently be such a poor judge of talent. Then, with the feeling that I was growing accustomed to, it occurred to me that it couldn't always be a matter of bad luck. Perhaps it was intentional. Perhaps Papa deliberately chose performers of lesser stature so that by comparison his own talent would appear much greater.

Several nights later I had dinner with Mr. Grossmann. Our correspondence had taken a firm, if still very new, hold, and in the late winter and early spring we had exchanged several short letters. For reasons I only partially understood, I had decided to keep the correspondence secret from Papa. It had not been difficult to do; I was the one who every day called at the front desk of our hotels for our mail. It was novel for me in that I had never before been inclined to purposely conceal something from him. The first time I did it, I felt guilty, but also independent. The second time, I felt only independent. So, when I agreed to dinner, it was natural not to mention it to Papa, who would be busy performing that night.

Although many fine restaurants and hotel dining rooms surrounded the Brunswick in Madison Square, when Mr. Grossmann arrived he suggested we go to the new Windsor Hotel, uptown at Fifth Avenue and Forty-sixth Street. "The atmosphere is a bit different from that of Madison Square," he said during the carriage ride there. "The Windsor is newer and brighter than the old hotels, and livelier. It attracts a large Wall Street crowd each night. If you don't like it, we'll go someplace else."

"I think I will like it," I said. Actually, I was interested in seeing this opulent new hotel, reputed to be the most modern and luxurious in the city.

The lobby and central dining room were crowded, but the rooms had been designed on so large a scale that the crowd was not overbearing. An air of good spirits and warmth predominated. Everyone, everywhere, seemed to be laughing, or at least smiling. Strangely, out of the many faces we passed, I could put a name to only one: Buck Grant, the son of the General, whom I had seen with his father in Booth's Theatre that night so long ago. This was unusual, for normally when I went out to a fashionable place in New York I encountered several people I knew at least by sight. Here, however, I knew no one. The group was of a business orientation, and Papa and I knew few people within it. I always prided myself on the scope of my social experience, having met so many of the influential and famous people of the world with Papa. Now, it struck me that my experience had been narrow.

Mr. Grossmann ordered from the elaborate menu, speaking to the waiter with the assured yet gentle tone of one secure in his social position. He was as comfortable in these formal surroundings as he had been that afternoon in the more casual German Beer Garden. I noted with admiration that his character was so well formed as to remain constant in social situations that differed widely. Perhaps I had lived my life too closely with theatrical people, where the ability to shift identities was valued, the very basis of art. How refreshing to be with someone who was as consistent and solid as Mr. Grossmann.

We chatted pleasantly during the meal. He told me of his childhood in Hungary, and of coming to America. "You have no idea how stultifying Hungarian society still is today," he told me. "And I speak as one who comes from the privileged class. The ancient class structures are still in place."

"Had you no desire to remain?" I asked thoughtfully. "No sense of nostalgia, of belonging there?"

"Indeed, there were many reasons to remain. In Hungary

I had a ready-made social position. As a descendant of land-owners, I was assured a comfortable life, with a fair amount of respect and privilege owed to me simply because of my birth. My life in Hungary would not have been unpleasant. But had I remained there, my true self would never have emerged. Only by leaving my past was I able to become my own man." He paused, smiling gently at me. "Of course, all of this must sound very odd to you, Miss Booth."

"Not as odd as you think." I was equally burdened by my family heritage.

The corridors, saloons, and dining rooms of the Windsor were even more crowded when we left than when we had arrived. The lively group gave every indication of planning to remain until very late in the evening. "They'll stay a while, although not much past midnight, as it's a weeknight," said Mr. Grossmann. "Most of these people must be in their offices early tomorrow."

Outside, it was one of those early spring nights with soft breezes full of the promise of the coming summer. "Shall we walk a bit to enjoy the evening?" he asked, and I agreed. Fortunately, I had worn a pair of good, comfortable shoes rather than the evening pumps, which would have made walking long distances virtually impossible.

We began a leisurely stroll down Fifth Avenue. Forty-second Street near Grand Central Depot seemed as crowded as it was in the daytime hours, with strollers out enjoying the evening and late commuters rushing to the station for the final evening train. The streets were nearly as bright as they were in daytime, thanks to the new electric streetlights. It seemed not to be nighttime at all, but the middle of the day.

I recalled that night when Downing and I had walked home from the supper party in Gramercy Park, the same party that

Mr. Grossmann had brought me to from Booth's Theatre. That nocturnal stroll had marked the real beginning of my relationship with Downing, the beginning of the path that had led to our engagement. That night I had felt elated, supremely happy. Now, I had nothing left but the knowledge of having experienced those feelings at that time. I could not recall the emotions themselves. I was glad of this, for it had been a path that led to nothing.

My thoughts made me silent for several moments, perhaps rudely so. "I'm sorry," I said. "I've been thinking."

"Yes?" he prodded, interested.

"About Downing."

He glanced at me to see if I was upset. But I wasn't; I could speak easily tonight.

"I've been thinking about him recently."

"That's natural."

"At first I couldn't. Then I thought so much that I feared I would go mad. Now, I'm finally sorting it out." I paused. "I think what we had was a match of falseness. But underneath, a part of me saw all along that it was false. He wasn't an artist, and never would be. And that is perhaps what attracted me to him. You see, as much as I've always said I wanted to be an artist's wife, a deeper, truer part of me never wanted it. Artists are very different from the rest of us, you know."

"Yes."

"Art can be a demanding thing. Sometimes those closest to the artist are destroyed, used up by the demand. That's what happened to my stepmother. She was simply crushed by it. I saw it happen, and a deeper part of me understood."

I stopped walking, and turned and looked up into his wide, gentle face. "Mr. Grossmann, please tell me honestly: Do you think me ill, or insane, to think these things? Sometimes I worry that my mind has become a little unhinged. I've had such terrible thoughts about Papa! I see such awful things about him, things that people would be appalled to hear. But I do believe they are true. Or is it that I am ill?"

His reply, plain and direct, came with no hesitation whatsoever. "No, Miss Booth, you are not. On the contrary, you are intelligent and perceptive, and that is precisely why you're now seeing these things. People in close proximity cannot help but learn things about each other. Unfortunately, we learn much that is not pleasant. And as you said yourself, artists are different."

An elderly couple passed us hand in hand. Mr. Grossmann politely lifted his hat, and I managed a little smile. I felt better having told him, and having heard his reassuring response. But I had fully expected him to respond in that manner. Less certain had I been of the attitude he would take toward Papa after hearing me voice negative thoughts about him. If Mr. Grossmann had become critical, or, worse, condemning, I would not have liked it at all; possibly it would have meant the end of our budding friendship. But he had not uttered a single judgmental statement about Papa, nor even gone so far as to agree with the remarks I had made. He had simply listened, accepted, and understood. "Poor Papa," I said, sighing deeply. "I do love him so much."

"Of course you do. He's your father. I have no doubt he loves you too."

"Yes, yes, he does! But he doesn't understand!"

"Understand what?"

"That I am different from him."

He was quiet a moment. "Then, Miss Booth, you must teach him."

"But how? How do I begin?"

"I'd say you have already begun."

"How?"

"You recognize that the problem exists, which is half the battle. Do you know how many people stumble blindly through life, unable or unwilling to see the flaws in those they love? Recognition is the greater part of the battle."

I fell silent again, considering this. It did sound plausible. Perhaps the worst was already behind me. Suddenly I felt an extreme sense of relief, and gratitude toward Mr. Grossmann for his insight. How wonderful it felt to have someone to confide in!

Having already walked half the distance back to the Brunswick, we decided to complete the trip on foot. When we arrived, he accompanied me into the lobby.

"We won't be returning to New York until the fall," I told him. "We summer in Newport."

"I usually go to Long Branch, with my brother's family," he said.

I'd been hoping to learn he summered in Newport also. The prospect of another long, reclusive stay at Boothden did not appeal to me at all. Why not invite him to visit? Quickly, before I could change my mind, I did. "The house is right on the Seaconnet River," I said. "I'm sure you'll enjoy it. We'd be so happy for you to come for a few days." He accepted graciously, and we agreed to write to each other later to arrange the dates. He shook my hand and said good night.

As soon as I was in my room I had misgivings about having invited him. Would Papa be annoyed that I had not consulted him first? He had sneered at Mr. Grossmann's commercial occupation. Perhaps when Papa came to know him, he would no longer feel that way. But even if he didn't change his opinion, what of it? Papa was too much of a gentleman to behave rudely to a guest in his home. After all, wouldn't it be a step in the right direction for Papa to understand that the same people might not appeal to both of us? Yes, I definitely wanted Mr. Grossmann to visit us this summer.

Later, as I was preparing for bed, I reflected upon the evening. Mr. Grossmann had been so sympathetic when I spoke to him of Papa, and his remarks had been so intelligent. How wonderful it was to have a friend again. My friendship with Julia had of necessity ended with her brother's departure from my life, for it would have been too painful and awkward for both of us if we had tried to continue it. But I could not deny that even before that I had begun to find her inadequate as a friend or confidante. Her buoyancy and good spirits, the very qualities that had attracted me to her in the first place, had begun to strike me as superficial and silly. But Mr. Grossmann seemed to offer qualities of friendship that were very real and substantial, much more attuned to the things in life that I was now finding important.

The next afternoon, a matinee day, I had just returned to my hotel room after visiting several bookstores in search of items for Papa when the bell on the telephone to the front desk rang. I picked it up, and the clerk informed me that Mr. Booth was asking if we were in.

"Mr. Booth?" I asked, bewildered. "Mr. Booth has a performance this afternoon. Are you certain of the name?"

I heard a muffled discussion at the other end. Then the clerk spoke to me again: "Mr. Joseph Booth." It was Uncle Joe! I said he should come right up.

While I waited for him to make his way upstairs, I felt a mixture of anticipation and apprehension. Why was he here?

Had Grandma Booth had an accident of some kind? Could Uncle Joe be ill?

The moment I saw him I knew nothing was wrong. He looked as well as he had the last time I saw him, or perhaps better. He looked younger, had even gained some weight, which served to increase his resemblance to his brothers. No matter what Papa thought, marriage obviously agreed with him.

"Papa's not here," I said as we went to the sofa and sat down. "It's matinee day. But you could stop by the theatre if you have to speak to him. He won't mind."

"It's nothing special," he said. "I can stay only a few minutes. I came on an errand, and have to return to Long Branch tonight. If I'm late, Margaret will worry."

"Uncle Joe, I'm so glad you're happy. Someday I'm going to meet Margaret, and I know I'm going to like her."

"She'll like you too."

"I miss coming to Long Branch. But maybe if we just give Papa time, he'll come around." The way Uncle Joe's face changed when I said this, his eyes narrowing, his lips tightening, told me that this was exactly what he had come to find out. I had suspected it as soon as he had mentioned Margaret, and I had tried to let him know as gently as possible that Papa's feelings were unchanged. "He needs more time," I repeated, even more gently.

But Uncle Joe's mood was too good overall for him to be fully downcast by this news. I asked if he would like something to eat or drink, but he declined. "I must go in a minute," he said. He reported on Grandma and Aunt Rosalie, who were both in reasonably good health. Then he stood up to leave. As we walked to the door, he suddenly said, "I came up to New York to see some people at New York University. I'm thinking of finishing my medical training."

"Uncle Joe, that's wonderful!" His inability to decide if he should do this had been for years a source of jokes in the family.

"Yes," he said. "I really should have a stable career to rely on. Especially now that I'm going to be a father."

It took a moment for this to fully register. "What wonderful news! When?"

"October."

"Congratulations! My best wishes, both to you and to Margaret." I paused. "I'll tell Papa right away. Right away—tonight."

"Thank you." He kissed me on the cheek and left.

A baby, I thought when he was gone. What a splendid thing to happen! The noise of a little child was exactly what was needed in that dreary house in Long Branch. Aunt Rosalie would be thrilled. Soon there would be another boy or girl with the last name Booth in the world. This was sure to change Papa's attitude toward Uncle Joe's wife.

Actually, I was surprised by my own reaction. Although I did not dislike children, I had never been particularly interested in them, at least not to the extent to which most women seemed to be. Honestly, I usually found young children boring and tiresome. I had grown up in a family without younger siblings, without cousins. As for the possibility of having children myself, I had never cared one way or the other. I was not averse to the idea, but neither was I especially eager. My goals in life had always been oriented differently, toward having an artist for a husband. But now things had changed, and I was amused that I found the thought of having a new little cousin so exciting. I couldn't wait to tell Papa when he returned.

———

"Yes, I know" was his response. His voice was sharp and cold. "Your grandmother wrote to me last week."

"Why didn't you tell me, Papa?"

"I chose not to. I wrote back to your grandmother asking that she not tell you either. I am very displeased that your uncle came here today and took it upon himself to tell you."

"Papa, is it necessary to be so harsh?"

"Yes."

"No matter what the problem was, surely people are capable of changing with time."

"Edwina, I know best in this matter. I am sorry for upsetting you. But this situation is a complicated one. In these family matters I must do what I believe to be correct, no matter how difficult that may be."

"Yes, Papa, yes," I said soothingly. I went to him and kissed his cheek. "Good night. Poor Papa, you feel things so much more keenly than other men."

"Good night."

I was delighted to discover that Papa would be hosting a breakfast for Henry Irving before we left New York. This was to be one of the final festivities prior to the return of Mr. Irving, Miss Terry, and the Lyceum Company to England. The idea, of course, had been Mr. Abbey's. Upon his arrival, Mr. Irving had been greeted by the prominent American actors Lawrence Barrett and William Florence. Now, when he was departing, was there any person in America more fitting to preside than Edwin Booth? Papa agreed at once. The breakfast was set for the morning of April 14 at Delmonico's, New York's premier restaurant.

Papa's quick agreement reassured me of his basic generosity

and magnanimity, things I had lately grown to doubt. There was no question that Mr. Irving was a rival of Papa's, a professional competitor. His spectacular success in America had been something of an embarrassment, especially since Papa had achieved nowhere near the same success in England. It would be only natural for Papa to be resentful and to wish to maintain a personal as well as professional distance from him. I myself was glad that Mr. Irving's tour of America was finished, and I would not have been surprised to discover that Papa agreed with me. Apparently, though, Papa did not feel that way; why would he have agreed to host the breakfast if he did? Since we had planned to leave for Boston on the very day of the breakfast, he could have offered the excuse of not being available. It was a relief to see the old Papa again, a man who was generous and good and had no trace of smallness or mean spirit.

The breakfast was for gentlemen only, as were so many of the private affairs at Delmonico's. Afterward, when Papa returned, I was eager to hear how it had gone. But he said little, other than that it had gone nicely and had been rather informal and relaxed. I decided that if I wanted to know I would have to wait until the newspapers came out; they would undoubtedly report on the event.

The afternoon paper carried a short piece. Papa had sat next to Mr. Irving. The guest list was long, and included some of the most prominent artistic, theatrical, literary, and political names in the city. All were men Papa considered his close friends, members of the social set with which he was most comfortable. I felt a flush of pride; Papa had seen to it that all of his close personal friends had attended the breakfast. He was truly a splendid man! I eagerly looked forward to reading the longer reports that would appear in the morning papers.

The next morning Papa had gone out by the time I came into the parlor for breakfast. Several of the morning papers he had been reading were still on the table, and I hurried over and picked up the one on top. In it I found a longer account of the breakfast. It gave the guest list, described the menu, and then went on to give particulars. At one point in the article Mr. Irving was quoted as having said that he regretted that he had not offered *Hamlet* in America. He would, however, be sure to offer it when he returned.

I put the paper down, a feeling of resentment starting to come over me. So we weren't completely rid of Mr. Irving. He was coming back, and he planned on doing *Hamlet* when he did. My resentment sharpened. *Hamlet* was Papa's play. More than any other piece, Americans associated it with Papa. It had seemed a mark of respect that Mr. Irving had not offered it during his tour.

I caught myself. What nonsense, I thought, for me to feel this way, jealous and resentful. I should really follow Papa's example. Papa's kind and generous attitude toward Mr. Irving was a splendid lesson in maturity and decency. It was something to aspire to.

I picked up another of the papers. Leafing through the large pages, I found the account of the breakfast. The top page included an artist's rendering of several of the guests attending. Papa's face was near the center, a flattering, younger version of himself. On the other side of Papa's picture a large, dark blue scribble completely blotted out the drawing of the face beneath. Papa had blotted Mr. Irving's face out of the picture.

For several moments I stared at the dark blue scribble. Then I folded the paper and placed it back with the others. I was no longer interested in reading accounts of the breakfast. My high spirits of the past few days were gone, deflated by the sharp point of the pen that had scribbled out Mr. Irving's face. Papa's air of generosity toward Mr. Irving was all an act, a performance for the public. An act that I had wanted desperately to believe.

My deflation of mood was not accompanied by a corresponding sense of depression. I felt a calm acceptance, and perhaps some pity. For what I was beginning to understand, with increasing clarity, was that the Edwin Booth whom the public saw was quite a different man from the jealous, threatened Papa who existed underneath.

SEVEN 1884

One morning in early May, Papa and I were finishing breakfast in our Boston home when, without looking up from his newspaper, he said in an astonished voice, "Fourteen million dollars."

"Papa?"

With a sigh, he folded the newspaper and put it on the table. "He'll never be able to pay it back, of course."

"You mean someone owes fourteen million dollars? It is a shockingly large amount. How unfortunate!" I raised my coffee cup for one last sip. "Who is it?"

"General Grant."

The cup nearly fell from my hand. "General Grant!"

He nodded. "Yes, it seems so. His son's brokerage firm failed. Grant was a partner. He's penniless now, along with all the other investors."

"Oh, no!"

"The worst part is that it failed because they were conducting business illegally." He slid the newspaper across the table to me. "Read for yourself if you're interested."

"Thank you. I am."

He stood up. "I must say, Edwina, you seem to be interested in all types of new things these days."

I took the newspaper as he left the dining room. There were

several reports, starting on the front page, and for the next hour I sat and read.

They were all more or less the same: The General had last year been added as a fourth partner to Grant and Ward, to give prestige to the firm. Ferdinand Ward, Buck's partner, was the financial brain, with a reputation that had a touch of the unsavory in certain circles. The third partner was a bank president, and the criminal activity had been collusion with that bank in using certain stocks as security for more than one transaction. Ward had already left the country, which was seen as an admission of guilt.

Most of the stories focused on General Grant, and the extent to which he had known of the firm's business practices. Many of them had headings such as GRANT: A CRIMINAL?

When I finished reading I dropped the newspaper on the table and pushed it away from me with the feeling that I had just seen one of Papa's tragic performances. It was all so very sad! I remembered the night I had sat in the box opposite the Grant family at Booth's Theatre, when I had envied them their good name, a name honored by all Americans. That name was now plunged into one of the worst business scandals America had ever known. To envy others their good fortune, or the security of their lives, was truly foolish, for such things were subject to change.

I could not believe that the gentle, kindly-looking man who had bowed to me in Booth's Theatre could be guilty. And how, I wondered, was Mrs. Grant responding to all this notoriety? What of Buck, who had drawn his father into the situation in the first place? For the first time I began to think that there might be worse crimes, more repugnant, than the one my uncle had committed. The crime that had become the scandal of the

Booth family had been rooted in political belief or mental illness, or both. But the crime that was at the root of the scandal now engulfing the Grant family had been greed.

I mentioned the scandal in one of my letters to Mr. Grossmann, who commented on it when he wrote back. He was aware of some things that had not been reported in the newspapers:

> How sad the entire situation is for General Grant! Many people in New York simply refuse to believe he could have known what was taking place, and I'm afraid I must admit I am one of them. I am willing to believe he was irresponsible, but not criminal. My feeling is equally strong about Buck. I have met him several times, and my personal feeling is that he is neither dishonest nor manipulative. I would hate to see either one of them prosecuted over this matter.

Shortly before we left for Newport I told Papa I had invited Mr. Grossmann to visit us at Boothden. At first Papa stared at me blankly, as though he had not understood my words. Evenly, I added that I hoped he didn't mind.

"Certainly I don't mind, Edwina," he said. "Boothden is your home as much as it is mine, and you are entitled to invite whomever you please. Of course Mr. Grossmann is welcome. He can stay several weeks if he wishes."

"No, he'll be staying for only a few days in June. He goes to Long Branch for most of the summer, to his brother's family. Apparently his nieces and nephews adore him and demand his presence."

We were in Papa's study, a large room on the ground floor of our home on Chestnut Street. The room was filled with furniture and objects. The walls, tabletops, and every available space on the shelves and mantelpiece were covered with souvenirs and mementos from Papa's career: a skull he had used in *Hamlet*, the four silver wreaths he had received in Europe, a rubbing from the inscription on Shakespeare's tomb, framed silk programs from his performances, small marble busts of Shakespeare and Goethe, and ribbons that had been attached to various wreaths. In a small frame on one table was the gold Tiffany's medal that had been presented to him for being the first actor ever to perform *Hamlet* for one hundred consecutive performances. All around were countless cabinet and carte-de-visite photos—pictures of his friends and respected colleagues. On his desk, facing him, was one small cabinet photo of me. The plain, simple photo looked overwhelmed by all the grand memorabilia around it. It looked out of place, as though it did not belong there.

Papa was sitting at his desk, large and of mahogany, on which several books were spread out. The one in front of him, I knew, was Shakespeare's *The Merchant of Venice*. Papa had decided to revive it in the fall, and had started work on his promptbook.

I had chosen to tell Papa about Mr. Grossmann's visit right after I gave him his morning mail, as I did each day. Now, I stood at the edge of his desk, holding the few pieces of mail that had come addressed to me. The morning was warm, and the study window was open. The heavy brown velvet draperies were barely stirring in the breeze. How rigid and immobile they looked! There had been no point in changing them for lighter summer ones, since the house would soon be closed up until the fall.

"Hmm," said Papa, leaning back in his chair. He took off his reading spectacles and looked up at me. "Of course, anyone you wish to bring to our home is welcome. I was just a bit surprised when you told me."

"I've lost touch with all my old friends from school, Papa. I'm trying to make a new friend. I like Mr. Grossmann."

"Yes, I remember you said you'd seen him in New York last winter."

"I did. We've been corresponding since then."

"I see," he said. He stared pointedly at the letters I was holding. "I see," he repeated. Suddenly I felt very uncomfortable and guilty. But I had done nothing wrong, I silently reasoned. I didn't have to tell Papa everything I did. I looked directly at him and smiled.

He smiled back. "Mr. Grossmann's in business, isn't he?"

"He's a partner in a stock brokerage firm on Wall Street."

"I didn't think business people took summer vacations."

I nearly laughed out loud. "Of course they do, Papa! It's not the same as the theatre, everything closing down in the summer, but business people do take vacations."

He put on his spectacles again. "I know little about such things. Well, it will be diverting to have Mr. Grossmann visit us for a bit." He went back to *The Merchant of Venice*.

Outside, I found a small letter from Mr. Grossmann. I had failed to notice it when first glancing through my letters. I opened it and read his confirmation of the dates he would be coming to Boothden.

Boothden looked and felt more settled this year. A large part of its sharp new quality had been worn away over the winter. The landscaping of the grounds seemed to have taken a firmer hold, so that they blended in with the natural surroundings, and the house itself appeared more solid, as though it too had taken root in the Rhode Island soil. Inside, the rooms no longer carried the vague scent of fresh paint and new wood, and the walls, floors, and ceilings flowed into one another smoothly. The entire estate seemed more of a unit to me, more used to itself, more comfortable with its existence.

During the last week in June, Papa and I drove into Newport to meet Mr. Grossmann at the train station. He had written that he would hire a carriage to bring him out to Boothden, but Papa said he wouldn't hear of it and insisted that we meet him ourselves. Papa, it seemed, was intent on making Mr. Grossmann feel welcome. I knew he was doing so to please me, but I couldn't help wishing he would just relax. Mr. Grossmann, after all, was my guest, my responsibility.

When Mr. Grossmann stepped off the train, he looked more or less the same as all the other passengers arriving for a summer visit. Nothing about him stood out. He wore a light summer suit and a straw hat, and he carried a nondescript suitcase. Yet I felt an excitement when I saw him, a sense of connection to the real world. He seemed to be an envoy from a place where people lived normal lives, lives that included families and well-ordered jobs, where emotions were direct and simple, not all spectacular and blown out of proportion. I was glad he had come.

I waved to him energetically. He saw us and hurried over. "Hello, hello," he said, shaking my hand lightly, then Papa's more vigorously. "It's so kind of you to invite me, sir," he told Papa. "I've been looking forward to this trip with great pleasure."

"We enjoy having guests," Papa replied. "That's one of the things a country house is for."

As we walked to the carriage, I noticed that Mr. Grossmann was several inches taller than Papa, and heavier. Papa, in fact, looked rather frail and small beside him. I would have to make sure he ate and rested properly during the summer. Such things became increasingly important as one got on in years.

I sat in the rear seat of the carriage, allowing Mr. Grossmann to sit up front beside Papa as Papa drove. This excluded me from the conversation, but as they spoke mostly of the progress of the career of Mr. Grossmann's brother, I was not particularly interested. Lately I was less and less interested in the theatre, and in things to do with the stage. At times I wondered if I had not always felt so but had been unwilling, as the daughter of a great tragedian, to admit it.

We were about a mile from Boothden when the carriage lurched suddenly to the side as one of its rear wheels jammed. The three of us climbed out to see what the trouble was.

"The wheel pin is missing," said Papa after he inspected it. "It must have shaken loose and fallen out. The wheel can't turn freely now. It keeps jamming against the axle."

"Let's look for the pin," I suggested. "It can't have fallen out too far back."

We searched the road for several yards back but did not find the pin. "There's nothing we can do," said Papa, with a small gesture of futility and a note of annoyance in his voice. "We'll have to walk the rest of the way. I'll send someone back for the carriage."

"Sir, if I may suggest," offered Mr. Grossmann.

"Yes?"

"If we could find a twig of appropriate size, one that's green and still pliable, it just might serve as a substitute for the pin and allow the wheel to move freely."

A crease appeared between Papa's eyebrows. "The carriage would still be too dangerous for us to ride in."

"Yes," I said. "But at least then we'd be able to bring the carriage home with us. Let's try it."

"Very well, we'll try it," said Papa. He looked blankly into the woods as if he had no idea how to start.

"I'll look for the twig," Mr. Grossmann said, setting off into the thick bushes on the side of the road. He disappeared from view, although his movements through the brambles remained audible.

Papa leaned against the side of the carriage, took a cigar from the small case he carried in his pocket, lit it, and then crushed out the match beneath his foot. "Quite an enterprising young man," he said as he exhaled a cloud of smoke. I nodded. Papa smoked far too much these days.

A moment later Mr. Grossmann returned, holding a twig. Propping his shoulder against the side of the carriage to lift just enough of the weight off the wheel for him to maneuver it, he adjusted the axle, then secured the wheel back in place with the twig. It was able to move freely under the weight of the carriage; the idea had worked.

"Well, well," said Papa. "It seems you were right."

"At heart, I'm really a simple man," Mr. Grossmann said. We were sitting on the bank of the river, where we'd strolled after lunch. "I want a good life, with material comforts, and I'm willing to work for them. But I've never wanted fame, status, or fortune. I think, perhaps, life's been easier for me because of this. I imagine that those things become terrible burdens for a man, especially after he's gotten used to having them. I think they build a wall, separating a man from others. To have so much more of something than everyone else must be terribly isolating. One must feel so much alone."

"Talent does it also," I said. "Great talent can be a terrible burden." I hesitated before continuing. "I think Papa is the loneliest man I know. He has many friends, but I don't know if he feels close to any of them. It's a double-edged sword, you see. The loneliness must be terrible, but there's a part of Papa that wants it that way. He's very competitive."

"Perhaps it's the need to stand out from the crowd. The need to be noticed."

"Yes, the need to stand alone."

"I've often wondered if that's what drives men to do great things, whether it be building great monuments, fortunes, or reputations. But do they not realize they must leave it all at death? How do such men face death?"

I thought of Papa asking me if he would die alone. "I don't know," I said. "Maybe some find it a relief, an opportunity to be free of their burden. Maybe it allows them to reconnect." Then I heard myself say, "The only person in the world I believe Papa feels connected to is me. And that is *my* burden."

As soon as the words were spoken, I was appalled that I had said them. How selfish I sounded! But I could not deny that they were true. "You must think me terrible," I said quietly. "To say that, given what I know about Papa's loneliness."

"Miss Booth, your father made that choice for himself. The burden is his. You have every right to release yourself."

"But you don't know," I said. My voice began to quaver. "He suffers such despairs, his black moods. It might destroy him."

"What might destroy him?"

"If he even suspected I resented him."

There was a silence. Suddenly I knew my resentment was the dangerous thing, not the wanting to have my own life. If I didn't make a life for myself away from Papa, I would eventually grow to hate him.

I could not underestimate Papa's strength, or his intelligence.

Finally Mr. Grossmann said, "He has survived much in his life. He will understand, eventually."

His tone drew me from myself. The way it had softened, yet deepened, added a rich dimension to his voice that spoke volumes. "You sound as if you speak from experience," I said.

"I do," he said simply. "I've had to leave things I've loved in order to be free. I loved teaching languages, but it prevented me from having things I wanted. Material things, I admit. I knew if I stayed I'd eventually grow to hate languages altogether, because of what I was denied. So I left. I still have my love of languages, but it has taken up a different position in my life. A smaller position, but one that preserves my joy in it. And I've acquired other joys from my new work, equal ones, that I would never have known had I refused to change." He rubbed his chin with his palm. "There have been other times also. There were people I loved in Hungary, family members and friends. Many were opposed to my coming to America, but I knew I had to come."

We stood up and began walking across the field back to the house. In the distance, we saw Papa on the porch of the house, looking as though he was on a stage.

The four days passed with astonishing speed. The evening of the final day we consulted the timetables for the trains leaving Newport in the morning, and determined that it was best for Mr. Grossmann to take one of the early ones. As the carriage had not been repaired, Papa would drive him to the station in the smaller buggy. It could accommodate only two, so I would not be accompanying them.

That night, when I went upstairs to my room, Betty casually asked me, "Your young man's leaving tomorrow?"

The phrase *your young man* caught my attention. "Mr. Grossmann's leaving first thing in the morning," I said. After a moment, I added, "He's not my young man, Betty."

"What is he?"

"A friend."

She gave me a quick, hard, skeptical look. "Don't play, missy. Enough people do that without you doing it too."

I stared at her. "What do you mean?"

"The way he looks at you."

I felt a tremor. "How does he look at me?"

Betty laughed. "'How does he look at me?'" she mimicked. Then she looked directly at me, her dark eyes fixing on my face. "There are a thousand things he wants to tell you, is bursting to tell you, but he's not sure he should. He's in love with you."

Incredulous, I was at a loss for words. Was she making fun of me, teasing me? But no, Betty had never done that to me and never would. Betty was the one person who always told me the truth. "You think he's in love with me?" I whispered.

"You'd better wake up, missy, 'cause that's not a bad thing at all. You could do a lot worse. This one wants nothing from you but you. Very different from that poor Mr. Vaux."

"That's enough about Mr. Vaux, Betty," I said sharply, more sharply than I meant to. But I was feeling very confused and disturbed, and it was coming out as irritability. More calmly I added, "Mr. Vaux was ill."

"He needed you. This Mr. Grossmann doesn't need you; he just wants you."

The floor seemed to have begun to move a little under my feet. I went to a chair and sat down. "I haven't thought of Mr. Grossmann as more than a friend."

"Well, you better start now. Make some decision about it. Stop playing a game. He's not the kind that plays games, or acts or pretends. It's not fair to treat him so."

Later that night I lay in bed wide awake, thinking of what

Betty had said to me. Of course it was the truth. It was my fault that I hadn't seen it. He was looking for a wife.

But it couldn't be me. I couldn't marry anyone. I was still confused about Downing, still confused about having almost married a man I hadn't understood. For years I had believed I should try to marry an artist.

The bedroom window, open and with curtains held back so as not to obstruct any breeze, was a bright rectangle of pearl-white moonlight in the darkened room. For the first time in many, many months I thought of my pearls that had been buried with Mama.

If only Mama were here with me now! Not Mama as she had been in the sad final years of her life, but the Mama I had known when I was younger, perhaps when I was ten or twelve. She had talked to me for hours on end in those days, and it had always seemed she had an answer to even the most perplexing questions I brought her. In those days before her illness had taken hold, there had been a practical, matter-of-fact quality to her that had helped cut through even the most confusing problems.

I sighed and closed my eyes. What would Mama say if I told her that I didn't think I could marry Mr. Grossmann?

And why is that, Edwina?

Because of John Wilkes Booth, I would answer.

I could see her pretty face frowning. *But what has he to do with it, dear?*

He is a burden, Mama. What he did is a burden. I should devote myself to service to try to make up for it. I shouldn't seek my own private happiness.

Edwina! Why should you be responsible for all that?

Someone has to be responsible. Papa can't bear it all. He has spent his whole life carrying the burden.

Oh, Edwina! Don't you know he likes it?

"Likes it?" I actually whispered. "Why on earth would he like it?"

Edwin's a tragedian. Being connected to a national tragedy in life helped him more than any publicity ever could have. A burden, perhaps, but much of it is his choice.

His choice! Why?

It helps people stay interested in him. People come to see his plays. But, Edwina, you have no reason for taking up that burden. None. You were not responsible.

I sat up, startled. Papa would not have become so famous if his brother had not assassinated Mr. Lincoln. I knew this was the truth as soon as I had thought it. I knew Papa too well by now to try to deny it. He wasn't aware of it, but an element of choice lay underneath his clinging to his brother's crime.

He had even used it to promote himself as a tragic figure. If it had been a burden for him at times, he had chosen to have it. And equally so, I could choose not to have it.

I lay awake in bed for a long time, thinking, while the bedroom seemed to grow even brighter in the moonlight. For me to consider Mr. Grossmann as a husband was still impossible. That had never been my intention; we were simply friends. It couldn't be anything more for far too many reasons.

I thought of him sleeping soundly in another room in the house. Instantly I saw his face before me, more clearly and vividly than I had ever seen anyone's before. He seemed to be drawn in bold lines, in strong colors. I recalled my constant difficulty with remembering what Downing looked like when I was apart from him during our engagement. In comparison to Ignatius, Downing had been a pale, wavering shadow.

Ignatius. Ignatius. I would have to get used to calling him

by his first name. Ignatius was not complicated or strange, the way Downing had been. He had no tangled motives, no sense of confusion about himself. He knew himself well, and what he wanted out of life. I saw with clarity who he was.

With him, I need not fear marrying someone I didn't know. Perhaps I could marry him.

Perhaps this was what I had wanted all along.

How unfortunate that he was leaving the next morning! I had wasted almost all of his visit. Then again, it was not completely wasted; I still had the morning. Thank goodness for Betty's plain speaking! Suppose Ignatius had gone away thinking I didn't care! He was so good, and so kind, and not at all unattractive. Yes, before he left in the morning I would find some way of letting him know of my feelings for him.

"I'd be very pleased if you'd call me Edwina," I said, permitting my hand to linger in his longer than usual as we said good-bye. The way his face suddenly seemed to brighten and the quick, reflexive tightening of his hand around mine at once removed any doubts I'd had about his intentions. Betty had been absolutely right. He was in love with me.

"Edwina," he said softly.

We were standing in the hallway, just inside the door. Papa had gone to bring the buggy around. All through breakfast I had waited for a private moment to speak with him, but Papa had always been present. I had almost despaired of the opportunity arising at all when Papa left us to get the buggy. That moment had turned out to be perfect.

We heard the buggy pull up out front. Reluctantly he released my hand. "Edwina," he said. "Thank you so much." He picked up his suitcase.

"Write to me, Ignatius," I said as I handed him his hat.

He looked a bit startled, hearing me use his first name. Then he smiled. "I will."

I opened the front door for him. Directly outside, the buggy was waiting. I watched him glide past me and out, then up into the seat beside Papa. Almost before he was seated, Papa gave the reins a tug, and the buggy pulled away.

I stood and watched as it disappeared down the driveway. He would write to me, and I would write back, and we would tell each other our feelings, hopes, and expectations for the future. We would begin to arrange our future together. Our letters this summer would be full of new plans. Then, in the fall, I would see him again.

He didn't write. One week and then another passed without my receiving so much as a short note from him. Of course, after the way I had behaved I could not very well write first. I had stepped over a certain social line by calling him by his first name, and there was no going back if I had been wrong. Could I have been wrong? With a horrible sinking sensation I began to wonder if I had once more misinterpreted a man. Had I, as well as Betty, been wrong in assessing his feelings? It didn't seem likely. The moment he and I had shared when he was leaving felt unmistakably clear. He seemed to care very much. Why did he now delay writing? I had fully expected to hear from him within a day or two after his departure. As the days passed with no word, I grew less and less optimistic. Every day I wondered if I had again been wrong in selecting a man to think of as a husband. Would I ever have the courage to make the attempt again? Perhaps I was truly destined to remain with Papa, unmarried.

Papa was behaving strangely. The day after Ignatius left,

Papa said to me, "Edwina, I think perhaps I've been wrong in not encouraging you to socialize more with young people."

"I'm fine, Papa," I replied.

"I noticed how much you enjoyed having a guest here. I think we'll have more company this year. You should go out more, into Newport with the young people. I hear they have very pleasant activities at the casino there."

"Oh, Papa, I don't care much for the people one meets at that sort of thing."

"Nonetheless, you should go."

I changed the subject. I did not want to explain to him that I had no desire to begin fending off the male attentions that such social involvement was sure to draw to me. The only man who interested me now was Ignatius.

True to his word, Papa at once began to accelerate our hospitality. Practically every day we had guests for luncheon or dinner. We began to meet all of our neighbors, most of whom were delighted to be invited to the home of Edwin Booth. In return, we received countless invitations to other homes, many of which we accepted. After a while I began to notice that the ones Papa wanted to accept were always to homes where he knew that young people would be present.

All this social activity, however, did little to alleviate my deepening misery at not hearing from Ignatius. When it reached three weeks from the day he had left, I broke down and confided in Betty. "He hasn't written," I told her. Struggling to hold back sobs, I told her how I had said good-bye to him, asking him to call me by my first name.

For several moments she said nothing. She stood very still, but I could tell that the wheels of her mind were spinning, calculating with her ruthless common sense. "Something happened," she said. "After he left you." She looked at me. "You got nothing from him?"

"No."

"Not even a thank-you note?" Her tone, and her expression, implied that she thought this was odd.

It *was* odd. In fact, it was extremely odd that he had been so rude as not to write to thank us for our hospitality. His manners were much too good for him not to know this was the thing to do. "Not even that. It's very odd."

"Write to him."

"Oh, Betty, I couldn't! It would be terribly inappropriate for a lady to take the initiative."

"No. Write and ask if he's sick." Betty hesitated, then added softly, "Missy, how do you know he didn't write?"

"Yes, it could have been lost! Or it … it …" My voice faded away as a thought occurred to me. I looked at Betty. She was staring straight at me, and the look on her face told me we were both thinking the same thing. Here at Boothden Papa received the mail first. He could have taken the letter.

The thought was appalling. Aghast, I started to say, "Do you think that …"

"Lost," Betty said firmly, and I understood. She knew all about Papa, all about his manipulative ways, but she would never utter one disloyal word. She understood and forgave him. Her understanding allowed her to protect herself from these things that could not be helped.

"Oh," I whispered.

"Lost," she repeated. "Missy, right now he may be wondering why *you* haven't written. Write. Ask if he's been sick. And tell the parlor maid to give your letters right to you."

———

Within a week, I was reading a letter from him:

Apparently my first letter failed to reach you. What an ingrate you must have thought me, Edwina, after you treated me so graciously on my visit! How insincere you must have thought me. If you only knew how upset I've been in thinking you had chosen not to resume our correspondence! Your father must think me despicable. On the way to the train station that morning I had gone so far as to hint that I hoped I might see more of you in the fall. I told him how highly I regarded you.

When I finished reading, I sat very quietly for a few minutes. A rage had built up in me as I read, a rage against Papa for what I was now certain he had tried to do. After Ignatius had spoken to him in the buggy, Papa had known an important letter would be coming. He knew what was developing between us, and he had tried to stop it.

Papa's sudden insistence on my starting to socialize began to make sense. Papa had been faced not only with the possibility of my marrying, but with the possibility of my marrying someone whom he did not like. Someone unlike Downing, someone who was strong and independent and whom he would not be able to dominate. Papa's insistence that I be with young people was nothing more than a campaign to distract me from Ignatius.

I forced myself to think of how Betty had been when she told me to write, her calm acceptance of this side of Papa. How deeply afraid he must be. Poor Papa! Yes, I could feel compassionate toward him. But he had to understand he could not manipulate me.

Should I confront him over the vanished letter? The thought of doing so made me shudder. Papa could only deny it or admit it, and either option presented a situation that was much too degrading for both of us. Of course, it was possible that the letter had actually been lost and that my imagination was running away with me, but it wasn't likely. With his distortions and lies and manipulations, Papa had in recent months given me every reason to believe that he had taken the letter.

I stared out over the field behind the house, down to the river. I did not want to have a confrontation; that would be cruel and might bring on his black mood. It would be far better for me to find a subtle way of letting him know that I knew, without actually saying so—a way that left some doubt as to whether I suspected him, but one that made it clear that the thought had at least occurred to me, and that if something similar ever happened again my suspicions would be confirmed. Such a way should not be too difficult to find.

"I received a letter today. From Ignatius."

"Who?" Papa did not even look up from his newspaper. We were sitting in the parlor after dinner, on a rare night when we did not have guests.

"Ignatius. Mr. Grossmann."

From the corner of my eye I saw him look up. I waited for him to speak, but he said nothing. I continued, "He especially wanted to thank you for exerting yourself when he was here."

"Hm," said Papa. "I see." The pages of the newspaper rattled as he turned them.

"Ignatius likes you so much, Papa." I spoke nonchalantly but stressed the name Ignatius.

I looked quickly at Papa; he glanced down at the paper, then up at me again. Returning my smile, he said, "A very pleasant man."

"He'll probably take us to dinner some night this fall, when we're in New York."

"How kind of him." Papa went back to reading his paper. I relaxed, knowing I had accomplished what I wanted to. In that brief moment when I had looked at him, before he had looked away, I had caught the worried look in his eye.

One evening near the middle of August, when Papa and I arrived home after a dinner engagement, he asked me to come into his study.

"Edwina, this came in the afternoon post. I said nothing earlier so as not to mar your evening." He held out a large white envelope. From where I stood I saw our address in Grandma Booth's large handwriting and a black border. I moved closer, and with trembling hands I took the envelope, slid the letter out through the side that had previously been opened, and read it.

It was short and to the point. Grandma Booth had written to say that Uncle Joe's wife, Margaret, had given birth prematurely earlier in the week. The child had died, and the next day Margaret had died of complications.

When I finished reading, I stood holding the letter, staring down at it. I thought of Uncle Joe, and how happy he had looked the last few times I had seen him, a happiness brought about by his marriage. He had been so thrilled at the prospect of becoming a father. Now, in an instant, it was all gone. The suddenness of it rendered it barely comprehensible and viciously cruel. It was unfair—terribly, monstrously unfair. Poor, poor Uncle Joe! I wished I could be there to comfort him, but any comfort I could offer would be woefully inadequate, utterly useless in the face of so tragic a loss.

"No one can help him," I said tonelessly.

"Yes, he was always that way," Papa said flatly. "He would never take advice from anyone. Stubborn and contrary, intent on doing things his own way. One of those men you can never reason with. In many ways as bad as Johnny." Papa paused, then added, "This entire incident of your uncle's marriage was unfortunate. Though I pity his suffering now, I cannot help but feel a relief that a situation I regarded as a mistake is over." Again he paused. "I must say I have deeply resented all the awkward circumstances that situation created. However, I now have every intention of forgetting all the trouble."

He came and took the letter back from me. "Tomorrow I will send him a brief note of sympathy. I'll include your name on it."

"No, Papa," I heard myself say.

He looked at me, surprised. "Edwina?"

"I'll write to Uncle Joe myself."

"There's no need for both of us to write."

"Yes, Papa, there is."

He continued to look at me, saying nothing. His expression was blank. I hesitated, but I was so utterly appalled by the things he had just said about Uncle Joe that I could not remain silent. Papa's attitude and the enormous unfairness that had fallen upon Uncle Joe had become the same thing, and while I could not protest the one, I could protest the other. It was essential for me to protest against Papa's cold and unfeeling side. I could not allow this moment to pass.

"I feel differently about Uncle Joe's marriage," I said firmly. "Differently from you, Papa. From the moment Uncle Joe became engaged, he was a new man. He went from being a sullen person whom I always tried to avoid to someone who was cheerful and glad to be alive. He looked happy, Papa!"

I paused for breath, then went on. "I'll write my own letter, Papa. Some things I have to say are different from what you'll be saying. I feel bad that I never met this woman who made him so happy." I stopped, debating whether or not to actually speak that which was now in my mind. "Papa, you love people, and I know how deeply. You loved my mother, and despite all the suffering, I know you loved Mama. No matter what you thought of his wife, Uncle Joe loved her. Try, just try, to imagine now the depth of his loss."

Papa remained silent, listening to me with an oddly empty look on his face. He did not attempt to interrupt or contradict me with so much as a change of expression. Then again, he had not stopped listening, turned away in anger, or walked out of the room. He stood and listened, as I would stand and listen to him now tell me how wrong I was, how I had misunderstood. I was prepared to face his great anger. I was not afraid.

For a long moment we stood facing each other. Neither of us spoke. We both needed time to adjust to the new circumstances in which we found ourselves. Around us the house was quiet, except for the slow ticking of the grandfather clock in the hall.

Finally he spoke. "You have the same nature as your mother," he said softly. "Loving, kind, generous, and so very forgiving. Above all, forgiving. When she died, I thought I would die also. I felt so completely, terribly alone." He walked over to where I stood. "I'd likely have gone mad had it not been for you." He sighed. "Good night, Edwina. Write to your uncle as you wish."

Papa's first theatrical engagement of the fall, at the end of November, was to be in Boston. When we returned to our home on Chestnut Street at the beginning of October I expected we would be there the entire fall. Right after Halloween, however, Papa told me he had to take a short business trip to New York and Philadelphia. I decided I would go with him. "On the day you visit Philadelphia," I told him, "I think I'll go to Long Branch and visit Grandma."

"What a nice idea," he replied. "I'd like to go with you, but unfortunately there won't be time."

So my long banishment from the Long Branch house was at an end. How unfortunate it was that only a tragedy could bring about my return! Would Papa, I wondered, really have come with me if time allowed?

I was also going to visit Ignatius, which was the primary appeal of the trip for me. Of course, I said nothing of it to Papa. I had been vastly disappointed that Papa had chosen to open in Boston again this year and would not perform in New York until January. That seemed an agonizingly long time to wait to see the man I was more and more every day hoping to marry. Almost six months had passed since I'd seen him. Even though he and I were exchanging at least one letter a week, and at times more, I worried that if we did not see each other his feelings for me might wane. With a keen sense of anticipation I wrote to him and made arrangements to see him upon our arrival.

Endeavoring to repay our hospitality of the previous summer, General Badeau took us to lunch the day we arrived. General Grant had reconsidered General Badeau's proposal to assist him in the writing of his memoirs, as Papa had suggested he might after the scandal of Grant and Ward. Although the uproar had died down, General Grant was penniless as a result, and the prospect of a best-selling set of memoirs suddenly seemed attractive to him. General Badeau moved into the townhouse on East Sixty-sixth Street with General Grant and his family to work full-time on them.

We sat down to lunch with General Badeau in the dining room of the Brunswick. His appearance was of a man a decade younger than the one I had seen last summer.

"Probably the benefits of a whole summer spent in the Adirondacks," he replied pertly when Papa mentioned how well he looked.

"More likely it's that Grant has agreed to do the memoirs," Papa said. His tone indicated that he meant it as a joke, and General Badeau did laugh with us, but I had no doubt this was much closer to the truth than the General's explanation.

"It's the same as the old days," said General Badeau, sighing happily. "We sit, talk, and work for hours on end. But it's sad, of course." He lowered his voice. "He's quite ill, you know."

"Really?" Papa asked gravely. "What's the trouble?"

"Cancer. He is not expected to live a year."

The words shocked me. "Oh, no," I murmured.

"Don't speak of it to anyone," General Badeau cautioned. "It was diagnosed only last month. It's a cancer of the throat. The doctors cannot do anything to eradicate the disease."

I thought of the kindly little man who had bowed to me that night in Booth's Theatre. In a few short months he had been subjected to public disgrace, loss of fortune, and now loss of health. Soon he would lose his life. At least Papa had been a young man when great calamity befell his family. He'd been allowed a lifetime to restore his good name and his fortune. General Grant now had less than a year. Life could truly be much crueler than it had been to Papa.

The waiter came to take our order. Mindlessly I chose something from the menu, although I seriously doubted I would be able to eat when it came.

"Will he be able to finish the book?" asked Papa.

"We hope so, but one can fade so quickly in these cases. Everyone, I believe, rests assured that if he cannot finish it, I will. I would be honored to do it!"

"Hm," said Papa.

Suddenly I was overcome with a feeling of intense dislike for General Badeau. His extreme good humor seemed inappropriate in light of General Grant's mortal illness. Did he have no feelings of sympathy or compassion for this man to whom he owed so much professionally? Was he aware of the man's intense suffering, or was he aware only of the possibility of great personal success that the situation offered him?

"How long has he been ill?" Papa asked.

"The first symptoms were noticed last summer when he was at Long Branch."

I stared at my napkin. It was so unfair, so very unfair. It was as if poor General Grant, who had done so much for America in the war, was finally being crushed by a terrible burden.

———

Ignatius and I had arranged to meet in a little restaurant on Twenty-third Street. I saw him as soon as I came in. He saw me at the same time, and hurried toward me. The sunlight from a nearby window, heavy and golden on this sunny fall afternoon, caught his head as he walked by it, and streaks of bronze glinted in his brown hair. "Edwina," he said softly, and I fought back a temptation to reach out and touch his hair.

He saw at once that I was upset. He led me to a little room in the back of the restaurant that had fewer tables, and we ordered coffee. "What's wrong?" he asked gently.

"He's dying," I whispered.

He frowned. "Your father?"

I shook my head. "General Grant."

A look of relief came over his face. Then he exhaled lightly. "There have been rumors of ill health."

"They are not just rumors. He has cancer of the throat." I told him what General Badeau had told us.

"Poor man," he said when I'd finished.

"I'm not sure why I'm so upset. It's not as though I really know him. I don't. But he was very kind to me once. There was a scene at Booth's Theatre that could have been ugly, but he stopped it."

The coffee arrived. I drank some and felt better. Then Ignatius said, "For one terrible moment I thought your father was ill."

"No, Papa's fine."

"He seemed healthy this past summer." He looked at me, his large hazel eyes now seeming to shine the way his hair had earlier. "It can't be half a year since I came to Boothden, can it? It seems only yesterday. Yet I assure you not a day has passed that I haven't thought of you."

I could only look at him and think how absolutely right it felt for me to be seated there beside him. Anyone else would have trivialized my being so upset over someone I didn't even know. Yet he had simply accepted it, the way he accepted everything. I felt as if I would be satisfied to sit there with him forever.

"I wasn't sure until you came in," he continued. "But as soon as I saw you, I knew I would have to. When I thought you meant your father was ill, it made me afraid—afraid that you might have a reason not to agree." He stopped speaking and lightly placed his fingers over my hand, resting on the table.

"Agree to what?" I asked, and he asked me to marry him.

Uncle Joe's house on Ocean Avenue looked smaller than I remembered, smaller and more worn and weather-beaten. Walking up the path to the front door, I wondered if it had always looked this way. The amount of time since I'd last visited, two and a half years, was not really long enough for a house to become decrepit. It was probably just that I was seeing things differently. This house, which had once looked so immense to me, was not half the size of Boothden or our home on Chestnut Street in Boston. With a pang of sadness I remembered that Boothden had in fact been built as a more suitable home for two of the occupants of this very house.

Aunt Rosalie greeted me at the door, and as soon as I saw her happy face I was glad I had decided to come after all. Since Ignatius' proposal the previous afternoon I had been in a state of emotional turmoil. I had passed a nearly sleepless night, and at dawn had wondered whether or not I should make the trip. Ultimately I decided that not going would not help me feel any better, and the opportunity to visit might not come again any-time soon.

I sat with Aunt Rosalie and Grandma in the parlor for a while, chatting quietly. Grandma Booth looked no different than she had a year before in New York, except perhaps that she moved even more slowly. Already pronounced, the marks of old age upon her had progressed no further. Aunt Rosalie, on the other hand, appeared to have aged terribly. She seemed to have prematurely stepped across the threshold from aging into old age itself.

The change in her could have been brought about only by the death of Margaret and her child. Aunt Rosalie must have grown close to her, living under the same roof for so long. The double loss of both her sister-in-law and the expected child had been devastating. Looking at her, I felt a twinge of dread. If the tragedy had brought about so severe a change in her, in what state could I expect to find my uncle?

Uncle Joe had not appeared when I came in, and neither Grandma nor Aunt Rosalie mentioned him. After an hour passed, I somewhat nervously asked for him.

"He's upstairs in his study," said Grandma. "He knows you're here today. You can go up and see him when you're ready. He probably won't be down for dinner. He doesn't come down much these days."

This frightened me, but I stood up. "I'll go see him now," I said resolutely. There was no point in delaying.

At the door of the parlor I hesitated. Uncle Joe had always been eccentric, and now he was suffering from the worst thing that had ever happened to him. I looked back at Grandma and Aunt Rosalie. "How is he?" I asked.

"He's grieving," Grandma said. She spoke with the quiet authority of someone who'd had an ample measure of grief in her own life.

"He burned all the toys," Aunt Rosalie whispered. "He was mad."

I looked at her, but she stared at the floor. My fear sharpened.

"The first days were difficult for him," said Grandma.

My legs felt shaky as I began to climb the stairs. What did *mad* mean? Was it the same as Papa's black mood? And if so, what could I possibly say or do to help him? I had been terrified of Papa's black mood ever since that one time I had caught a glimpse of it as a child. I had no understanding of it. I did not know how to confront it, and now here I was on my way to face Papa's brother.

Why should I be so afraid? Mama had certainly been mad, and I had managed with her. I had been angry with her at times, but never frightened. And Downing? People had whispered that he had gone mad. I had comforted Downing better than anyone else. It was illness only, illness of the mind or emotions. *Illness* was a far less frightening word than *madness*. Illness could be managed.

I took a deep breath. Upon opening Uncle Joe's door I would think of him as ill, not mad. With that decision I was no longer afraid. When I reached the top of the stairs, the closed door of the study loomed before me. Don't be afraid, I told myself, and I tapped lightly on the door.

I heard footsteps coming. The door swung open, and I was face to face with a haggard, pale, bearded version of my uncle. He wore a crumpled flannel robe. His narrow face was almost white, and there were dark circles beneath his eyes. With a sense of enormous relief I saw no trace of that extinguished quality I had seen in Aunt Rosalie. Something had died in Aunt Rosalie; some spark of life had been snuffed out. But in Uncle Joe, although the marks of grief and deep despair were all over him, life still remained. Why he had survived his much greater loss and his sister had not survived hers, I did not know. But he had survived it in some fundamental way of which she was incapable.

"Hello, Uncle Joe." I stepped into the study. The door swung shut behind me.

The room, originally intended as a bedroom for servants, was narrow with a low ceiling. The sparse furnishings were mostly second-hand items. Books were crammed nearly floor to ceiling. At one end a huge, overstuffed armchair, extremely comfortable-looking in spite of its ragged appearance, had been pulled up in front of an old wooden table, which apparently served for a desk. How different it was from Papa's elaborate study in our Boston house.

A coal fire was burning in the grate, but it was insufficient to cast the chill out of the room. I shivered involuntarily. Wordlessly, with a series of quick, jerky movements, Uncle Joe went and threw more coal from a nearby pail onto the fire. Then he dumped some books off a wooden chair, the remnant of someone's dining room furniture, and placed it next to the grate. "Thank you," I said as I sat down.

He dropped into the armchair behind the table. For a moment there was silence. How should I begin? I had seen that he would survive his tragedy, but it was evident that his grief was still raw. Finally I said simply, "I'm sorry, Uncle Joe." He glanced at me and then reached over to the table.

"Did you get my letter?" I asked.

He nodded. After a pause, he began to stir through a pile of papers on the table. At last he pulled something out and held it up. I recognized the letter I had written him from Boothden last August. I stared at the pile of papers. Were they all letters of condolence he had received?

"I meant everything I wrote in that letter, Uncle Joe," I began. "Every word of it. I'm so sorry I never met Margaret. She must have been wonderful, absolutely wonderful."

He put down the letter and picked up something else from the table. With a swoop of his arm, he reached across and offered it to me. I took it; it was a cabinet photograph of a woman. "Margaret?" I asked, looking at him.

"Yes," he said.

The woman looking up at me was not beautiful, nor was she very young. She was a trifle overweight; the words "pleasingly plump" came to mind. Her eyes were set a bit too closely, and her nose was large. But she was smiling one of the most beautiful smiles I had ever seen, a smile that seemed to indicate that her entire being was filled with happiness and joy. Margaret smiled in the same way as Ignatius.

Something cold and hard seemed to clamp down on my heart. "Damn Papa!" I suddenly heard myself say, my eyes beginning to sting as they filled with tears. "He had no right to act the way he did! He had no right!" All the frustration and tension of the past day seemed to crest inside me. It was followed by a great flood of tears. With one hand I covered my face while in the other I clutched the photograph of Margaret.

Uncle Joe stood up. Through my tears, I saw that his face was utterly startled and confused.

"I'm sorry, I'm sorry," I managed to mumble between sobs. "I should be comforting you, I know. It's just so unfair that Papa took the attitude he did." Again the thought overwhelmed me, and my throat constricted. My shoulders began to heave with my sobs.

Uncle Joe darted past me to a shelf. A moment later he was pushing a small ceramic mug filled with liquid into my hand.

"Drink it," he said, and I did. It was some kind of alcohol, and burned my throat as I swallowed it.

When I was finished, he pressed a clean white handkerchief into my hand. I wiped my eyes, blew my nose, and took a deep breath. The drink had landed in my stomach with an explosion of warmth, and I felt its effect at once.

"What was that?" I asked in a thin voice.

"Whiskey. Good medicine, sometimes. I've had plenty lately."

I handed the photograph back to him. "I wish I'd met her. Papa was so wrong not to let me visit." My voice became harsh again as I said this.

Uncle Joe heard it too. "What's wrong?" he asked gently. He sat back down in his chair. But he did not drop listlessly into it the way he had earlier. He sat upright, looking at me attentively, his face full of concern.

"I've no right to burden you with this," I said, my voice quavering. "You're the one who's suffering now."

"Margaret's gone and there's no helping it," he said. "But something seems to be terribly wrong with you. Maybe we can do something about that." He paused, then added quietly, "I've known your papa longer than you have, if he's the problem."

"He is!" I cried, and even though I started sobbing all over again, I managed to begin telling him about Ignatius.

"... and now he's asked me to marry him, and I don't know what to do."

"What was your answer?" Uncle Joe was leaning far back in his chair.

"I told him I couldn't say yes until I was ready to tell Papa. He said he would wait as long as I need him to. He would never pressure me; he understands all about Papa. But will I ever feel ready? This is one problem that can only get worse with time. It'll be worse six months from now, or a year. I'm afraid that if I don't tell him now, I never will. I'll just grow old caring for him, waiting for him to die. What a horrible thing that would be."

I looked at Uncle Joe, ready to see the condemnation in his eyes for my voicing such an awful thought. But he said only, "Then it would be too late for you anyway."

He picked up the photograph of Margaret. Swiftly he touched it to his lips, in a gesture that was almost heartbreakingly sad. "She used to come here and sit right where you're sitting now. We'd talk about all the things we were going to do. I'd finish school, become a doctor, maybe move to New York."

"Uncle Joe, why did Papa dislike her so? She appears to be the type of person no one could dislike."

"I never found out."

"Really, you can tell me. I won't be shocked or hurt. A year ago I might have been, and three years ago I certainly would have." I could even smile a little at the memory of the girl I had been. "I probably wouldn't have believed you. But not now. So, please, tell me."

He lifted a hand helplessly. "I have nothing to tell. Truthfully, I don't know."

"You never asked her either?"

"I chose not to. For me to do so would have been, in a way, giving in to Ned's manipulation. All along, you see, I had a suspicion it was nothing, or almost nothing. I'd seen him take odd dislikes to people during the time I worked for him at his theatre. It was most likely no more than that. So I decided not to trouble myself about it. Besides, the real problem, of course, was my not doing what Ned wanted me to do."

His words struck a chord within me that resonated; they were true. An odd feeling of mixed relief and anger presented itself—relief that most likely no real reason existed for Papa's hatred of Margaret, and anger that he had made so much trouble about it for all of us. His hatred of her was nothing more than a spark of a whim, fanned by his need to control people and his fear that he would not be able to.

That same need was the very reason why he disliked Ignatius. He understood he would never be able to control him, just as he had not been able to control Uncle Joe. And if I married Ignatius, Papa would also understand he could not control me either. Not anymore.

Slowly I said, "Yes, I see that about Papa. He needs people to do what he wants them to do. He only does it because he's afraid. What I saw as anger in him about you and Margaret was really fear." I hesitated. "And it comes back to something I've known for a while about him."

"What?" he asked gently.

"He's afraid he will die if I leave him."

"I'm not surprised. That's what happened when he left our father. He's worried about retribution," Uncle Joe said.

I stared at him. "What happened?"

"To put it simply, Ned finally managed to break away from Father. For years he'd been serving as his keeper, going everywhere with him, caring for him in his madness. But when they went to California Ned decided he'd had enough, and was staying. He refused to leave when Father decided to return East. Father died on the trip back."

Something in my mind fell into place, and at once I understood. I remembered that night I found Papa on the steps behind Boothden. When he asked me if he would die alone, I assumed he meant it as a question of whether family members would be present at his death. What he had really been giving voice to at that time was a deeper fear, the fear of living alone. "How did my grandfather die?" I asked.

"He drank the water of the Mississippi River. Ned always felt if he'd been there he could have prevented it."

My old feelings of protectiveness toward Papa arose. "He wasn't responsible," I said firmly.

"Certainly not. But you see, right after that he came to be viewed as Father's successor. Ned doesn't see it, but in some ways he's actually lived our father's life for him. He stepped into his shoes. Johnny could never get over it. He wanted those shoes for himself."

Slowly I said, "Is that why he—"

Uncle Joe sighed and leaned back in his chair. "I think it was underneath. Ned had won, Ned would always be first. Johnny and Ned had chosen opposite sides in the conflict between the states, and Johnny felt strongly about it. When the North won, it was just one more time Johnny lost. In some way he mixed up Lincoln-the-victor with Ned-the-victor. He felt crushed, like the South."

The fire in the grate had died down, and the room was growing cold. Without asking, I got up and threw the remaining coal into the grate. I felt lightheaded and dizzy. Many thoughts swirled through my mind, finally finding their proper places.

"Your father won't die if you marry this man," Uncle Joe said. "He won't like it, but he won't die."

My back was to him; I stared down into the fire. "But the black mood," I whispered.

"He'll get through it if it comes. He's gotten through it before. Don't you see what will happen if you let him deprive you of your happiness? My advice is this: Grab your own chance of happiness. You can make others happy only if you're happy yourself. Ned will get through it. He's gotten through so much else in his life."

Papa wouldn't die. He would get through it. He wouldn't like it, but it wouldn't destroy him. I thought of this repeatedly on the train ride back to the city. I was exhausted, and the problem was not over. Indeed, I was still frightened of facing Papa. Yet I no longer had the sense of hopelessness and helplessness I'd had before my talk with Uncle Joe.

The first thing I was going to do was tell Ignatius I would marry him. I would commit not only to him but to my happiness as well. Then I could delay only so long before telling Papa. It would not be pleasant, but now I could tell him.

So much of what Uncle Joe had said about Papa's competitiveness with his younger brother John Wilkes rang true. Papa had crushed John Wilkes. It was completely consistent with some of the unpleasant things I had learned about Papa in recent years. His domination occurred on subtle, nearly invisible levels, levels that were apparent only to the close observer. Not until I left St. Mary's and began to live year-round with Papa and Mama did I see how he exerted control over everyone around him. Had anyone else ever suspected these truths? I recalled my conversation with General Badeau at Boothden about Papa and his brother. Now I could see that the General suspected something comparable to what Uncle Joe had told me. But General Badeau would never speak of it. The world would never know that at heart John Wilkes Booth had been a little boy who had felt crushed by his older brother. I would not allow myself to be crushed. I would marry Ignatius. I leaned back on the seat and felt a sense of resolution.

When I arrived in Jersey City I left the train and took the ferry across to Manhattan. It was already dark, and I went directly to the small hotel where Ignatius lived. The concierge told me he hadn't yet returned from his office, so I sat down to wait in the lobby.

About ten minutes later he came in, greeting the concierge pleasantly, still cheerful at the end of the day. "Ignatius," I called lightly.

He whirled to look at me, and I rose and went to him. "I'll marry you, I'll marry you," I quietly sang.

He pulled me into his arms and laughed. "Right now? Tonight?"

I laughed too, and felt the tears in my eyes. "No, in the spring."

He stepped back. "Your father?"

"I'll tell him soon."

"I'm not rushing you?"

"No."

He pulled me forward and, for the first time, kissed me. His lips were soft and moist on my own, and felt comfortable, and so very right. Our lips parted, and we both stepped back, then looked into each other's faces. He smiled. I had not been mistaken in seeing the same expression on the face of Uncle Joe's wife.

"I'm going to marry, Papa. I'm going to marry Ignatius."

He stared at me, not understanding. "Ignatius? Who is Ignatius?"

"Mr. Grossmann."

His eyelids half closed over his dark brown eyes as comprehension settled into them. For a moment he didn't speak but simply stood looking down at me. Then he slowly sat down on the sofa beside me. "I see," he said quietly.

"Oh, Papa, I've been so afraid of telling you."

"Afraid? Why afraid?" His voice was calm, very controlled.

"Afraid of hurting you. I don't want you to be lonely when I leave—"

He held up a hand to stop me. "No," he said, and seemed about to say more. But he hesitated, as though he couldn't find the right words.

"Papa, I know you're not comfortable with Ignatius, but when you get to know him better—"

"Edwina," he said. He reached over and took my hand in his. "Edwina! None of that is your concern. It's for me to be concerned with your happiness, not for you to be concerned with mine. Now, Edwina, listen to me very carefully. If you love this man and wish to marry him, then of course you must do so. I would never, ever stand in the way of your happiness. I want only what will bring you happiness. Edwina, it appalls me to think you feared telling me this!"

"Perhaps I didn't need to, Papa." I stood up. "It's late. Tomorrow I'll tell you more. We'll sit and have a long talk about it."

"Yes, yes, tomorrow," he said, standing up as well.

In the morning I could scarcely believe I had done it. Papa's reaction had been so wonderful that I couldn't wait to write to Ignatius to tell him. Of course I had some fear about the effect it would have on Papa when he grasped it fully. At least I had done it. I had taken the step I had been so fearful of taking.

At breakfast I noticed that Papa looked pale and haggard, as though he'd passed a sleepless night, but he spoke to me in frank, encouraging terms. "I won't deny, Edwina, that this is not the man I would have chosen for you. It does seem a rather odd match to me. Yet I have no doubt of his basic decency and integrity as a gentleman, and I have no opposition to the marriage if you love each other."

"We do, Papa."

"I must admit I was rather surprised, for it does seem sudden to me. I thought your friendship with Mr. Grossmann had lapsed after his summer visit. I believed you had discovered yourselves incompatible after that time together. Apparently I was wrong."

The incident of the missing letter came into my head, but I pushed it out. This was an enormously difficult time for Papa, a time that called for understanding, not bitter memories. I smiled at him. "We've been corresponding frequently. I saw him last month in New York."

"How soon do you wish to marry?" he asked, suddenly tense.

"I was thinking about next May."

He relaxed visibly. "Not so soon, then."

"No. There's time to prepare. Of course, I want to be married here in your home."

"Yes, by all means."

"That makes everything much easier. You didn't have this beautiful house when I was engaged to Downing. Then I felt overwhelmed at the thought of the preparations. Now it all seems so much easier."

Gently he said, "It's hard to imagine someone more different from Downing than this man."

"I've changed, Papa. I know myself much better now than I did when I wanted to marry Downing. My experience with Downing caused me to grow. I've learned so many things."

"We must view our difficulties so," he said in a strange voice. "We must learn from the tragedies in our lives."

"We must learn to be happy."

For the rest of the morning I felt a giddy excitement. Papa stayed in his study throughout the day, emerging only briefly for a quick lunch, then returning right away. I didn't disturb him. I suspected that he was thinking about my plans, and I hoped that his initial good reaction was not going to change. It would take time for him to fully realize the magnitude of the change that was coming in his life. I shouldn't press him faster than he was prepared to go.

As soon as we sat down to dinner that night he brought up the subject. "Edwina, this house is so large. Do you think you and Mr. Grossmann might care to live here?"

I had known this question would come. I said, "We'll have to live in New York, Papa. Ignatius works there."

"I see."

"New York isn't so far from Boston. You could always take a flat near ours. None of this has to be decided right away, Papa. It's still half a year until the wedding. Then, of course, we'll be away on our honeymoon trip for several months."

The mention of a trip took him by surprise; clearly he had not thought there would be one. A startled look appeared on his face, and the hand holding his dinner fork trembled slightly. Then he composed himself. He smiled. "Have you decided where you'll be going?"

"We'd both like to go to Europe."

"Really." He paused, then said, "That surprises me, since you've been twice already."

"We'll be going to different countries. Ignatius wants me to see Hungary, where he was born. Besides, Papa, those trips were not happy times for me. Mama was ill during the first one, and Downing during the other." I was drifting into areas I didn't wish to be in. "We've talked about going to Spain and Italy also, countries I've never been to."

"That will be quite a trip," he said softly. "A long one."

"Yes. So you see, Papa, there's no need to rush into any decisions about your future living arrangements. That can wait." *Until you're better used to the idea,* I added mentally.

"Your mother and I went to Niagara Falls for our honeymoon," he said distantly. "We always spoke about taking a trip to Italy. She died before we could."

Talk of death and dying was to be avoided at all costs now. "I think my mother would approve of Ignatius," I said. "Mama did. Do you remember that time she met him after you opened in *King Lear*? It was so strange the way she took to him that day. That was the first time I met him."

"I don't remember," Papa said.

After dinner he left for his performance. I did not wait up for him; I seldom did when we were at home in Boston. Before retiring I wrote another short letter to Ignatius, telling him how well Papa was continuing to take the whole matter. I wondered as I fell asleep how often people spent their lives worrying about things that would never occur.

Papa was not downstairs when I entered the dining room for breakfast the next morning. The table, I saw, had only one place set. Time seemed to be suspended as I stood staring at the ominously empty chair. Had he already finished and gone out on some errand? I rang for the maid.

"Mr. Booth's not feeling well, miss. He will not be down for breakfast," she told me when she came in.

In an instant my sense of well-being came crashing down

around me. The smooth, empty whiteness of the tablecloth before his empty chair confronted me mockingly. Papa was not sick physically. The black mood had arrived. I fought back a wild urge to run upstairs to Papa's room and plead for forgiveness. I heard the maid asking me if she should bring my breakfast now. I started to tell her no, for I was too anxious to eat. *This is going to kill him,* I thought dully. Then I remembered Uncle Joe. The very thought of him was calming, a mental balm that was strengthening.

The maid was staring at me. "Yes," I said firmly. "Please bring my breakfast now." I would need to fortify myself. "Large portions, please; I'm hungry this morning. Strong coffee also. Please tell Cook to prepare a tray for Mr. Booth. I'll bring it up when I've eaten."

Half an hour later I stood with the tray outside the door to Papa's room. In my pocket was the spare key, in case it was locked. "Papa?" I called as I knocked lightly. "I've brought your breakfast." Then without waiting I turned the knob and went in.

So many thoughts had run through my mind in the past few minutes, so many memories. I recalled how frightened I'd been in Long Branch as I climbed the creaky steps to Uncle Joe's study, not knowing what state of mind I'd find him in. As I entered Papa's bedroom, I remembered entering Downing's room in the hotel in Berlin. I'd been so grateful to find him alive, yet so horrified by the condition we found him in. Now, when I looked down on the bed and saw Papa lying there on his back, looking small and fragile among the pillows and sheets, I thought of Mama the last time I saw her. More than any of the others, this last memory clawed at me, and my eyes began to moisten. It wasn't the same, though. Papa would become well again. He was overwhelmed right now, oppressed by depression. But he would be well again.

"Edwina," he whispered feebly.

"I've brought your breakfast, Papa," I said. I placed the tray on the table next to the bed, then went to the window and drew back the drapes. Harsh, bright winter sunlight poured into the room.

His arm flew across his eyes. "Daughter ... please ... too bright ..."

I drew them half-closed. "Better, Papa?"

Slowly he removed his arm. He blinked two or three times, then said in a low voice, "I'm sorry. The bright light hurts my eyes." Deep lines creased his forehead, but his eyes remained open.

"What's wrong, Papa?" I placed my hand on his forehead to see if he was feverish, but his skin was cool to the touch. "Shall I call the doctor?"

Ever so slightly, he shook his head no.

"Then I think you should eat something. I've brought two nice soft-boiled eggs and some toast and coffee."

He winced as though the notion of food was intolerable to him. "Papa," I said firmly. "Tell me what's wrong."

A long sigh escaped his lips. "So difficult to explain."

"Try."

"Oh, Edwina, I feel the hand of death upon me!"

It was time to stand up to him. "Papa, you feel that way only because your father died after you left him."

He closed his eyes as if to shut out the very thought of what I was saying. But I had spent half an hour preparing myself for this confrontation, steeling myself, and I was not going to stop. "Yes, you were your father's companion for years," I continued, "and right after you left him he died. I've been your companion, and now I'm leaving, and you think it's some kind of retribution, some sort of punishment you deserve, and that you have to die. Well, Papa, I'm sorry, but I must tell you: I've never heard anything so silly in my entire life!" I went and stood directly over him. "Papa, your father died from drinking contaminated water. Even if you'd been with him, you couldn't have prevented it."

An image began to form in my mind of Papa as a young man in his teens, struggling to care for an erratic, unstable parent, traveling with him, devoting his youth to caring for him. Wasting his youth. Suddenly I was angry. "Papa, it was wrong that you were the one caring for your father. Simply wrong! You, hardly more than a boy! You should have been in school, or playing! To think that you blamed yourself for that old man's death! Why, it's the most ridiculous thing I've ever heard!"

I folded my arms and looked down at him. He was staring at me, his eyes fully open for the first time since I entered the room. Had I said too much? I certainly hadn't intended to say all those bitter things, and yet they were what I honestly felt, and I couldn't regret having said them.

I dropped down on my knees beside him. "Papa, Papa, I must go on with my life, find my own place. For me that's something different from what it's been for you. I'm not one of the people who're supposed to make a great difference in the world. I've always known I'd never be an Ellen Terry or a Mrs. Howe, but for a long time I felt I had to devote myself to someone important. But that's wrong, Papa. I want different things. I want a long, happy marriage. I want children, and a permanent home for them. And I want privacy."

I took his hand. "I have to make my own life now. But, Papa, your life will continue as usual. Edwin Booth is still Edwin Booth."

I felt a light pressure on my thumb as he squeezed it. "Papa," I said, "there's an audience waiting to see you tonight. Can't you at least try to perform for them?"

For several moments he said nothing. His eyes remained open, staring up at the ceiling. I knelt there silently beside him. It was useless for me to attempt any further persuasion or argument. Either he understood or he didn't.

I had almost given up hope when I noticed that the pressure on my thumb was growing much stronger.

He turned his head toward me. "Well, bring me those soft-boiled eggs," he said. "Maybe I can swallow them."

His performance that night was splendid. Half an hour after he left for the theatre I followed him there. I sat in the last row of the orchestra section, ready to run backstage at the announcement that Edwin Booth had been taken ill and could not complete the performance. But there was no announcement. Afterward I thought his performance as Shylock that night was one of the best I'd ever seen him give. His grief in the scenes where he lamented the elopement of his daughter was so poignant that many people in the audience, myself included, were moved to tears. When the final curtain came down I raced out and back home, and greeted him there when he returned.

The days that followed were difficult for him, but he was clearly making an effort with his melancholy, and the blackness of his mood shifted to gray. After a week the worst of the despondency had subsided. It was time for Ignatius to come visit. I wrote and asked him to come the next weekend.

"It seems, sir, that you have captured the heart of my daughter," were Papa's first words to him when he arrived.

"The most splendid heart in the world," Ignatius replied.

They talked in Papa's study for more than an hour. I waited in the parlor, anxious and excited but not afraid. When they finally came out, they both looked serene and satisfied.

"We must have some champagne now," said Papa, and rang for the maid. Behind him, Ignatius winked at me. All was well. The situation I had been dreading for so many months had come about without disaster. After Papa had made a toast to our happiness, he no more than touched the glass to his lips and did not even take a sip of the champagne. He was struggling valiantly, but it would take some time before the black mood was completely gone.

NINE **1885**

"A letter from your father," said Ignatius, holding it up for me to see as I came down the wide staircase in the main lobby of our hotel. I reached the bottom, and he handed it to me. "It's postmarked July 21, so there'll be nothing of Grant's death in it."

News of the death of General Grant on July 23 had reached us at Lake Como in the Italian Alps as quickly as it had reached parts of America, but the details were much slower in coming. For the past several days since we'd heard, we had sought out whatever scraps of news we could find. Ignatius, knowing of my special fondness for the old General, had been concerned that his death might affect my enjoyment of our honeymoon, which up until this point had been blissful beyond my expectations. The news, though, had not disturbed me or brought on a mood of melancholy. I was glad that his suffering, which had been considerable, was finally ended, and that he was at peace. Yet I did wish to read the accounts of his death that would appear in the American newspapers. I was curious to see how the life of this great man had been brought to its conclusion.

Ignatius and I were preparing to spend the morning driving through the countryside. "Why don't you read your letter while I see about our carriage," he suggested. "It will take me a few minutes."

He went off to the stable, and I wandered toward the terrace.

The hotel was just outside the town of Bellagio, set amidst the splendid scenic attractions surrounding Lake Como. Stepping outside, I paused to marvel at the crystal-clear quality of the air in the region. This morning the sky was solid blue, as it had been every day since we had arrived from Vienna. It was perfectly matched by the placid, glassy surface of the lake spread wide before it. No wonder the region was one of the most popular resorts in Europe.

The terrace was empty. It was still early, and I had my choice of the many wooden armchairs set about it. I chose one at random and sat down. I hesitated a moment before opening my letter, addressed to "Edwina Grossmann" in Papa's heavy, firm hand. Papa and I had corresponded regularly since my departure. He seemed to be responding to my absence well, after an initial melancholy, which, although he had tried to conceal it, had seeped into his letters. After he had gone to Boothden and had begun receiving his summer guests there, the tone of his letters had changed, with the underlying sadness almost completely vanishing.

Now, as I looked at the envelope, I felt a twinge of anxiety for the first time in weeks, the old worry for Papa's well-being. He was so far away, beyond an ocean, on the other side of the world. Perhaps Ignatius and I should cut our trip short, return to America without visiting the rest of Italy. Sternly, I made myself break off this train of thought. The death of General Grant must have brought it on. I opened the letter.

It began, as always, with Papa's expression of missing me, and then went on to a general statement of his health. Then he reported on his friends and acquaintances—those he'd been seeing, those he was corresponding with. This particular letter was full of information about Grandma Booth and Aunt Rosalie, both of whom were in declining health. They had recently moved to New York City with Uncle Joe, who had proceeded with his plans to enter medical school. Papa helped them make the move, and I was pleased to know that much of the animosity of recent years between him and Uncle Joe was gone.

Oddly enough, the next part of his letter did pertain to General Grant. His memoirs had been completed, were said to be splendid, and were having an astonishing advance sale. Papa wished to know if he should order a copy for me. Of course, he reminded me, I should not mention it to General Badeau if I saw him in the future. His work with General Grant had not gone well, and he had been replaced on the project.

When I finished the letter, I again felt a moment of the old anxiety, the old concern. Would I ever cease to worry about Papa?

I looked out over the lake, into the distance where rose the foothills of the Alps, which looked majestic, dramatic, and picturesque against the sky. Behind them were other mountains, mountains that were high and dangerous and difficult to climb.

I thought of Aunt Rosalie, whose life had withered away. I thought of Downing, crushed by his father. I thought of Mama, overwhelmed and overshadowed by her husband, and of John Wilkes Booth, by his brother. I thought of Papa as a boy, struggling beneath the weight of a mad parent. I thought of all these things, and it seemed to me that against all odds I had somehow managed to escape that which they had not.

I got up and walked to the hotel's front entrance. Ignatius was waiting there with a little buggy for our sightseeing excursion.

"How is your father?" he asked as he helped me in.

"Fine."

"You know," he said as we pulled away, "we don't have to go on through Italy if you'd rather return home."

"Ignatius, I've waited many years to see Italy," I replied after a moment. "Nothing in the world could make me turn back now."

THE END

A NOTE ON SOURCES

"Booth's Daughter" is a work of historical fiction. The events around which Edwina's story has been built—such events as Edwin Booth's acting tours, Edwina's engagement to Downing Vaux, the death of Edwina's stepmother, the building of Boothden, Edwina's marriage to Ignatius Grossmann—actually happened. For some events about which not much is known—the death of Joseph Booth's first wife and child, for instance—a story has been constructed from the scant information available. In a few places, minor facts have been adjusted or changed in support of the plot or themes. Dialogue, excerpts of letters, and newspaper clippings are all fictitious.

The following sources were especially helpful for writing Edwina's story:

SOURCES

Brennan, John C. "John Wilkes Booth's Enigmatic Brother Joseph." *Maryland Historical Magazine*, Spring 1983.

Grossmann, Edwina Booth. *Edwin Booth*. New York: Century Co., 1894.

Hatton, Joseph. *Henry Irving's Impressions of America*. Boston: James R. Osgood & Co., 1884.

Howe, Julia Ward. *Reminiscences, 1819-1899*. Boston: Houghton Mifflin & Co., 1899.

Kimmel, Stanley. *The Mad Booths of Maryland*. Indianapolis: Bobbs-Merrill Co., 1940.

Lewis, Lloyd, and Henry Justin Smith. *Oscar Wilde Discovers America*. New York: Harcourt, Brace & Co., 1936.

Lockridge, Richard. *Darling of Misfortune*. New York: Century Co., 1932.

McCabe, James D. *Lights and Shadows of New York Life*. New York: Farrar, Straus and Giroux, 1970.

McFeely, William S. *Grant*. New York: W. W. Norton, 1981.

Paine, Albert Bigelow. *Mark Twain*. New York: Harper & Brothers, 1912.

Ruggles, Eleanor. *Prince of Players*. New York: W. W. Norton, 1953.

Samples, Gordon. *Lust for Fame*. Jefferson, N.C.: McFarland & Co., 1982.

Watermeier, Daniel J. *Between Actor and Critic*. Princeton, N.J.: Princeton University Press, 1971.

The Encyclopaedia Britannica and *Valentine's Manual of Old New York* were also consulted.